The LOTTERYS
More or Less

The LOTTERYS
More or Less

EMMA DONOGHUE

illustrated by
CAROLINE HADILAKSONO

HarperCollinsPublishersLtd

FOR OUR DEAR FRIENDS
LIZ, TADHG, AND LORCAN VEECOCK
AND SINÉAD MCBREARTY,
BECAUSE, AS THE PROVERB SAYS,
WELCOME IS THE BEST DISH ON THE TABLE.

CHAPTER 1
THE SHORTEST DAY 1

CHAPTER 2
PARADING 35

CHAPTER 3
THE LONGEST NIGHT 55

CHAPTER 4
THE ICE STORM 79

CHAPTER 5
GOOD KINGS WENCESLAS 113

CHAPTER 6
THE PLUNGE 143

CHAPTER 7
BITTER WEATHER 179

CHAPTER 8
AMIGO SECRETO 217

CHAPTER 9
FOOD, GLORIOUS FOOD 249

Once upon a time, a man from Delhi and a man from Yukon fell in love, and so did a woman from Jamaica and a Mohawk woman. The two couples became best friends and had a baby together. When they won the lottery, they gave up their jobs and found a big old house where their family could learn and grow . . . and grow some more.

Now Sumac Lottery (age nine) is the fifth of seven kids, all named after trees. With their four parents, one grandfather, and five pets, they fit perfectly in the Toronto home they call Camelottery.

But the one thing in life that never changes . . . is that sooner or later things change.

MaxiMum

CardaMom

FREE SHRUGS

Wood

Catalpa

Sic

Chapter 1

THE SHORTEST DAY

"We just need some snow, and then the holidays will be perfect," Sumac tells Grumps.

"Oh, aye." Her Scottish grandfather doesn't look up from his crossword. Crosswords are meant to be good for dementia, which is the thing that muddles Grumps's brain.

The two of them are up in the Artic — what the Lotterys call their attic for doing art, on the very top floor of their house. Grumps is not doing any art; he's just being company for Sumac. She's cutting a crescent moon out of aluminium foil to make a shadow picture in her lantern. "Tonight's the Solstice Parade," she tells him. "That's what we're making these lanterns for, remember?"

Grumps's pale blue eyes look suspiciously vague, which means he's probably forgotten what the Solstice Parade is.

Sumac has an idea: She picks a giant square of cardboard out of the pieces stored behind the cabinet, and starts making a holiday calendar.

This time last year Grumps was probably celebrating in a sad-old-man way with a slice of cold turkey, listening to the radio in his little house in Yukon. He's never been at Camelottery in December, so he doesn't know what's coming — what a perfect mix of different kinds of fun it's going to be. Well, perfect if the snow will just fall like it's supposed to.

Sumac writes:

December 21   Winter Solstice
               (shortest day of year!)

               Bye-bye to Luiz (our couchsurfer from
               Brazil)

               Ice Sculpture Fest

               Solstice Parade

Before Luiz turned up, Sumac was expecting a woman called Louise, because that's what his name sounds like (and the website's profile picture of him was backlit and blurry, so you really couldn't tell), but he's actually a boy. Well, a man — though *nineteen* still has *teen* in it.

She adds a little drawing of herself at tonight's parade, with her moon lantern (lit up by an LED light) bobbing on a long bamboo pole.

"*Solstice Parade*," Grumps reads over her shoulder. "Is that one of those makey-uppy, New Agey things?"

"Actually, people have been celebrating the longest night for thousands of years," says Sumac. Or does she mean millions? "Stonehenge," she adds — not quite sure how old that famous stone circle in England is, but people definitely sun-worshipped there. She carries on with her festive calendar, which has got as far as tomorrow.

December 22   PapaDum and Sic get back from Delhi in time for:

The Nutcracker

Saturnalia Banquet

Sumac hasn't been thrilled about one of her dads spending nearly the entire month back in India turning a factory on the outskirts of Delhi into free apartments for homeless

3

people. Especially because PapaDum took Sic with him, even though her big brother's only sixteen and knows zero about construction.

Tomorrow, though, all Lotterys will be together at *The Nutcracker* (Sumac's favorite ballet) before coming home to recline on couches for their ancient Roman banquet.

The sky outside the Artic window has that flat white look that just might mean snow. Sumac crosses all her fingers for luck to make it fall this afternoon and cover up the gray ice heaps studded with cigarette butts and doggy dirt, turning everything creamy and new in time for Christmas.

Grumps is pointing at where it says *Saturnalia*. "I had a Saturn."

What's he on about? Saturn's a planet. And the Roman god of money, Sumac remembers. . . . Or is it time? So how could her grandfather have had a Saturn? A little statue of the god, maybe? But when people with dementia say random things, you're not supposed to annoy them by contradicting them, so Sumac just nods and draws icicles on the capital letters of *Ice Sculpture Fest*.

"A Saturn Astra," says Grumps.

"Mm, white, wasn't it, Dad?" says PopCorn, standing in the door of the Artic. "With those nasty fleece seat covers."

"They were very practical when I was driving around in the Yukon snow," Grumps tells his son.

Oh, so a Saturn must be some kind of car. Sometimes Sumac forgets that there are moments when Grumps's memory works just fine.

She knows her dad is probably here to check up on Grumps discreetly, but he's always helpful with crafts too. "I'm making a calendar of festivities," she tells him, holding it up; the cardboard's nearly too wide for her hands to grip the edges.

"Splendid idea," says PopCorn.

"Can you do a picture of the Nutcracker with his helmet and his soldier's jacket?" she asks. *The Nutcracker*'s about a tool for cracking nuts, shaped like a toy soldier, that comes to life. "I tried, but he looks like Homer Simpson."

"Happy to be of use." PopCorn grabs the black, red, and gold felt-tips.

"The snow really has to start falling by tonight," Sumac tells him, "or our holidays won't be half seasonal enough."

PopCorn sniggers.

"What's funny?" Sumac asks.

"You, bossy-boots, trying to tell the weather what to do."

She sets her mouth in a horrible scowl.

"Oh, lovely," he says. "Let me draw *that* on your calendar."

Sumac makes her face smooth again.

PopCorn carries on coloring in the Nutcracker's uniform. "I can't believe Luiz is off on his travels already."

"Who's that?" asks Grumps, looking up from the paper.

"You know, Dad — the lad who's been staying in our Overspill in the basement."

"Eats all the bananas," says Grumps sternly.

"No he doesn't," says PopCorn.

"He does, actually," says Sumac, amused that Grumps has noticed.

Luiz was PopCorn's idea — or not Luiz in particular, but the idea of welcoming in couchsurfers who can't afford hotels. PopCorn loves sharing, like tool exchanges where you lend your neighbors lawn mowers or yoga slings, or swap meets where you give away pumpkins if you've grown too many, or turn people's old sweaters into bags.

"He's been here three days and he's had about twelve bananas," Sumac reports. Actually, she hasn't seen much of Luiz, because he stays out half the night at *meet-*

ups and *mingles*, and sleeps in half the day, and takes lots of showers.

"Fish," Grumps mutters over his crossword.

"What was the clue?" Sumac asks him.

He shakes his head.

"You mean you want fish for dinner, Dad?" suggests PopCorn.

"Visitors," Grumps snaps. "They're like fish."

Sumac tries to think of why that could be. Slippery?

PopCorn clicks his fingers. "It's a wise old proverb. *Guests, like fish, stink on the third day.*"

You'd think Grumps would be pleased that his son figured it out, but he just grunts.

This morning Sumac is studying the winter solstice by looking up astronomy websites in the moms' bedroom — so MaxiMum can explain any hard bits while she's polishing her shoes.

From the look of this room, you'd think the two mothers didn't suit each other at all, rather than being nearests and dearests. MaxiMum's side is all neat and monkish, but CardaMom's is all messy, with scattered scarves, and jewelry dangling from nails in the walls.

"What I find interesting," says MaxiMum, "is that the earth's actually at its nearest point to the sun right now, but that doesn't make us any warmer."

Nearest point? Sumac frowns. "Isn't an orbit a circle, like when you swing something around on a string?"

"Slightly oval," says MaxiMum. "We're a hundred and forty-seven million kilometers away from the sun, give or take a hundred thousand or so, whereas in the summer we'll be more or less a hundred and fifty-two million kilometers away."

"Why do you say *give or take* and *more or less* instead of the actual figures?" asks Sumac.

MaxiMum grins. "Go look up the actual figures, then, you pedant."

Pedant's like *fusspot* or *nitpicker*. These things her family call Sumac just mean she likes to get details right, so she tries not to take them as insults.

"But remember there's always a margin of error," MaxiMum adds, taking the brush to her best Italian leather shoes now.

"What's a margin of —"

MaxiMum cuts in. "The chance that the scientists could be a bit wrong. Say, plus or minus five percent."

An alarm beeps on her phone.

"What do you have to do?" asks Sumac.

8

"Call the dentist to make twelve appointments for our checkups," says MaxiMum with an irritated sound. "*Another thing PapaDum usually takes care of. You don't realize how much a coparent does until he's out of the country.*"

Sumac comforts her: "He'll be home tomorrow."

MaxiMum sends Sumac off with a challenge: to explain the seasons to Brian (who's four), using household objects.

Hm. What kind of objects should Sumac use? Books? (Her favorite objects.)

Plastic tubs?

No, fruit.

Sumac goes two floors down to the Mess (the Lotterys' kitchen) and ransacks the bowl. First she gets a grape for the earth and an apple for the sun. Then it occurs to her that the sun is *way* bigger than the earth, so she looks it up on one of the family's tablets and finds that it's actually 109 times as wide. Because she can't think of a fruit 109 times wider than a grape, Sumac ends up borrowing a huge melon (the long green-and-yellow stripy kind called Santa Claus melons) for the sun. And an orange pip (dug out of the slimy compost tub on the kitchen counter) for the earth.

She tracks Brian down in the Loud Lounge upstairs. Brian is tucked behind one of the four sofas, in her polar bear earmuffs, of course. (She got them at the start of

9

December and has been wearing them night and day ever since.)

"Want to know about the seasons?" Sumac asks. She waits. "Brian? If you can't hear me through those things, take them off."

"I can hear," says Brian. She doesn't look up from the two tiny cars she's driving in figure eights over a huge beanbag. "Winter, summer, springer."

Sumac corrects her: "Winter, spring, summer, and *fall*, actually."

"Fall*er*."

Sumac doesn't argue, because (a) that's going off-topic and (b) Brian won't put up with being corrected. For a person so small, Brian's always very sure. Like last year, when she was three, and announced she wasn't a girl, and changed her name from Briar (the tree name the Lotterys gave her when they adopted her) to Brian.

"But what makes the seasons different from each other, do you know?" Sumac asks, as excitingly as she can.

Brian drives one of her little cars up on top of the other.

"Sure you can hear me through your polar bears?" asks Sumac.

Brian nods. "Just not listening."

That makes Sumac grin. She pushes a pin down through the orange pip, then says, "Look, this pip's the earth."

Brian holds up her cars squeezed together like a sandwich. "Look, double-decker bus."

"Right," says Sumac. "So the earth pip is tilted away from the sun melon at the moment. We live on the top half —"

"Where?" asks Brian, squirming closer.

Sumac finds a black marker and adds a dot to the sticky pip. "There, that's us in Camelottery, in Toronto, in between the five big lakes, in Canada, in North America."

"But where?" Brian's buzz-cut head, with the two polar bear heads covering her ears, is only a few centimeters away from the pip. Maybe she expects to see little Lotterys crawling about like fruit mites if she squints hard enough.

"We're on the top bit that's angled away from the melon right now," explains Sumac. "So the light from the melon — from the sun — we get it for less time every day than people down at the bottom in . . . South Africa, say."

"Lions." Now Brian steers her cars around each other over a big rubber exercise ball, making a motor sound in her throat.

"That's right! The lions are having nice long days, lying around in the sunshine, whereas we're shivering."

Brian's cars slam into each other and fall off the rubber-ball mountain onto the carpet. She makes explosion sounds, her tiny fists shooting out fingers.

Sumac checks: "So do you get it about the seasons?"

"Sun be always there?" demands Brian.

"Ah, pretty much always, yeah." Sumac happens to know that the sun's middle-aged, so in about five billion years it's going to go out like a match. But that's far too far from now to worry about, and the information would probably freak out a four-year-old.

"Want slice of the sun," says Brian, patting the melon, which sounds like a drum. "And me cutting." She's got her penknife out already.

"We need the big chopper in the Mess for that," Sumac tells her. "Let's go ask somebody."

"Somebody!" roars Brian on the landing. "Slice of the sun!"

The two of them find their couchsurfer in the Mess, still having his breakfast, with banana skins and earbuds and espresso cups spread all around him. And he's sprinkling sugar on an avocado: bizarre.

Luiz is so short and skinny, he looks way younger than nineteen. *"Bom dia, amiga!"* That's Portuguese, which is what they speak in Brazil. He leaps up to greet Sumac with his usual two air kisses.

Sumac stiffens with the effort of remembering which way to dip, so she and Luiz bash noses.

He yelps, then grins, and rubs Sumac's nose better.

"Sorry," she says, "I remember that *right is right* but I keep forgetting whether it's *my* right or *yours*."

"You go to my right cheek and I go to your same," he says, demonstrating on Brian.

So, aim left, Sumac decides.

"Look for you carry that big thing, Brian!"

Luiz has never had any English lessons; he's just watched a lot of YouTube.

Brian grits her teeth like a weightlifter, heaving the melon up above her head to show her muscles.

Sumac remembers something and checks her watch. "Aren't you supposed to be gone?" That sounds rude, so she adds, "I mean, isn't your flight — wasn't it eleven this morning?"

Luiz is flying to Paris (France) via Munich (Germany), which means going east and then backtracking west, because for some strange reason that's cheaper.

"Is OK, later." He flaps his hand in a *whatever* kind of way and sits back down, taking a big scoop of sugared avocado.

This must be like what CardaMom calls Indian Time: doing things when they should be done instead of by the clock. It doesn't come naturally to Sumac, who's worn a watch since her third birthday. "But Luiz, you've missed your plane now, and they won't let you on the next one!" Her voice comes out squeaky. Can their couchsurfer even afford to buy another ticket? Right after he left Rio, the real — that's what they use there instead of dollars — *fell to a four-year low*, a thing Sumac still doesn't understand even after CardaMom explained it twice, but basically it means Luiz's savings for his trip got shrunk, like laundry if you wash it in very hot water.

Luiz lets out one of his honking laughs, like a drain coming unblocked. "No, I mean my plane is later," he tells her. "Before, I read the hour wrong. Is eleven this *night* actually. So I see beautiful Canada one extra day."

Toronto's really not that beautiful this week, it's pretty gray. Sumac feels bad that the Canadian climate isn't doing its proper White Christmas thing for Luiz, with fluffy snow and all.

Brian is starting to stagger under the weight of the melon. "You cut me slice of the sun?"

"Yeah yeah, no biggie." Luiz reaches for it and Brian lets go a second too early —

The sound the melon makes on the wooden floor is an awful, heavy, wet *smush*.

"Desculpe," cries Luiz. That's what Brazilians say when they're sorry.

"We broked the sun!" Tears jump out of Brian's eyes.

"No biggie," says Sumac back to Luiz, just to be polite.

"It is *very* biggie," Brian wails.

"The real sun's fine," Sumac reminds her, pointing out the window at the sky.

Luiz is laughing regretfully as he takes a selfie with the mess.

"Let's put the pieces in the compost," Sumac tells Brian.

"Dibs cut them with my knife," says Brian, sniffling.

Sumac puts three big crushed chunks on a chopping board for Brian to practice on. "Slice away from yourself, yeah?" She's afraid for those little fingers.

Luiz starts mopping up the floor. He's better at cleaning up than her big brothers. He picks up the melon's little label: "From Brazil, like me."

Aspen slams her way in from the Hall of Mirrors. "Opal just pooped on the floor, and I got some in my wheel!"

It feels to Sumac as if her sister's been wearing those Rollerblades all December, and the thump of her wheels never stops. "Why did you ride through the poop, though, rather than around it?"

"I was being a scientist," Aspen boasts, "and testing the con — con — constancy."

"You mean *consistency*. That's gooiness or hardness," Sumac tells her. "*Constancy* would mean if Opal poops on the floor *constantly*, which he totally doesn't."

Aspen does that creepy thing where she mimes pulling a thread to lift up just one scornful corner of her upper lip. At nine, Sumac knows way more words than Aspen, but she has to admit that her sister (at ten) knows more grimaces.

PopCorn hurries in with Opal the parrot perched on his shoulder. "Paper towels, please — we don't want Oak sliding around in that."

Sumac snatches the roll of paper towels off the counter and tosses it to PopCorn.

Their brother Oak's getting around pretty fast these days, by crawling or cruising from one piece of furniture to another, and his latest craze is painting himself with anything he finds, like toothpaste or guacamole or . . . anything disgusting.

"Where be the poop?" asks Brian.

"Dirty bird," Aspen scolds Opal.

The parrot screams, "Kapow!" (Their brothers Wood and Sic are always teaching him silly words.)

"It's only because he's pining for PapaDum off in Delhi, so his tummy's upset," Sumac tells Aspen.

PopCorn hurries away to clean up the poop, with Brian right behind him.

Parrots are one-person pets, really, so it's bad luck for Opal that he's ended up in a twelve-person gang. Still, Sumac guesses he prefers the Lotterys to the smugglers who kidnapped him, anyway. Opal's left wing hasn't worked ever since he was rescued from a suitcase full of baby African gray parrots at Toronto's airport.

"FYI, his poop's nearly black instead of the usual green, look." Aspen lifts one Rollerblade to show it, which makes her tip backward with a crash, knocking the mop out of Luiz's hand.

PopCorn comes back in, holding the parrot low so Brian can stroke Opal's downy head. "Poor bird. One more day and our beloved PapaDum and Sic will be back," he promises them all.

Yeah. Sumac needs her funny, smarty-pants, eldest brother (who likes to call her Smackeroo) as much as her most patient, solid, never-too-busy-for-a-hug father.

"Blades off, now, poppet," PopCorn tells Aspen, "and go wash every speck of guano out of your wheels. So, Luiz, here's a bit of snow for you at last."

Sumac spins around to see. In the Wild behind Camelottery, white specks are spiraling down.

"Ave Maria Mãe de Deus!" Luiz plucks his really thick glasses out of his scattering of possessions on the table and jams them on his face.

Sumac's never seen anyone so excited by a little sprinkle of snow — or no adult, anyway. Oak was like that last winter, goggling and blinking as the flakes landed on his cheeks.

"In Rio we always wish for the snow but it never . . ." Luiz lunges toward the back door.

"You're in flip-flops," Sumac reminds him, but he's racing across the Derriere already — slap, slap on the boards of the porch — and jumping down onto the grass.

"He says Brazilians can do anything in flip-flops," says Aspen, "even play soccer and climb mountains."

"Now, who's supposed to be rustling up some lunch?" asks PopCorn.

Sumac makes an effort to remember. "You and Catalpa are," she tells him.

"We cut up the sun but it smushed," says Brian.

The three parents and four bigger kids have been taking turns to cook this month, and not very well. For seventeen years PapaDum's been master of the kitchen, as well as house repairs, so the rest of the adults have gradually lost whatever of those skills they once had. (The same goes for other departments: These days MaxiMum decides pretty much everything about the garden, CardaMom's the only one who remembers the passwords for electronics, and PopCorn's in charge of creativity because he went to art school for six months.)

PopCorn leans out into the hall now and wails, "Catalpa!"

A faint cry: "What?"

"I need you."

Catalpa — fourteen and exhausted-looking in an elegant way — stomps down from her room.

"Co-chef, did we have a concept for lunch today?" asks PopCorn.

"Yeah. You said you'd make red rice pilaf."

PopCorn groans.

Sumac's stomach growls. Red rice takes forever.

"Change of plan," says PopCorn, throwing open one of the two refrigerators. "Ring the cowbell for lunch, Brian, will you? Hold on to your hats, folks, because it's Deli Sandwich Delight!"

That sounds great until you realize it just means he's going to plonk cold things on the long table, wave like a magician, and say in an unconvincing Southern drawl, "Go wild, y'all."

Brian seizes the cowbell and shakes it violently for quite a while.

The clang brings MaxiMum downstairs. "Thanks, that's enough," she tells Brian, and stops the clapper of the bell. She starts putting out plates and glasses.

Next comes their middle brother, Wood, talking Grumps's ear off about the longbow he's made, and how next he'd like to try a crossbow.

"Where are CardaMom and Oak?" Sumac wants to know.

"Still boogying at the physio's," says Catalpa, shaking back her long black hair with one of those yawns that implies everything is tedious.

"I had a physio," says Grumps resentfully. "Made me tightrope walk and pretend to be a flamingo."

This puzzles Sumac: forcing old people to walk on tightropes, really?

Oak goes to physiotherapy to work on making his left arm and leg as strong as the right ones. (He's more like a one-year-old than a two-and-a-halfer, because somebody shook him when he was tiny, before he and Brian came to Camelottery.) Sumac went along to help him once, and it was mostly dancing with multicolored water bottles and — for some reason — looking in mirrors.

Sumac makes herself a cheese sandwich, which is not exactly *going wild*, but she likes cheese sandwiches. Sumac's bio-dad's ancestors are German — she's Filipina on her bio-mom's side — and the Germans are the fourth-biggest cheese eaters in the world after the French and the Icelanders and the Finns. Sumac adds baby carrots to her plate, and tries not to look at Aspen helping herself to corned beef and raspberry jam between two garlic crackers. (Yuck!)

Their grandfather is staring at the table. Too many choices muddle his brains.

"Cheese sandwich, Grumps?" suggests Sumac.

"Don't mind if I do."

So she makes him one just like hers, except with mustard.

"Did his physio really make him walk a tightrope?" she murmurs to PopCorn.

"No, no, just walk a straight line as if it was a tightrope," he tells her, miming it.

Whew, that sounds a lot less dangerous.

Wood takes nothing but dead pig: wet ham, dry ham, pepperoni, and salami. He stares out the window at Luiz, who's still cavorting in the snow in his flip-flops. "Has anybody called the dude in for lunch?"

"He only just had his breakfast," explains Sumac.

"He better enjoy the snow while it lasts, because it's going to turn to freezing rain," says Wood gruffly. At twelve, Wood's voice hasn't actually changed yet; he just tries to make it sound manly. Recently he's become a weather nerd, always going on about gusts and flurries, depressions and subtropical cyclones.

"Freezing rain?" echoes Sumac, horrified. "For the Ice Sculpture Fest and the Solstice Parade?"

"Yeah, duh, because the gods have never been known to be cruel before," says Catalpa.

"Don't fret, petunia," PopCorn tells Sumac. "What do those weather forecasters know?"

"Quite a lot more than you," murmurs MaxiMum, who's on the side of the scientists, because she used to work in a lab.

"Last winter we got such a dump, Grumps — twenty centimeters overnight," Wood tells their grandfather. "We built this amazing snow fort in the Wild behind the house, with flying buttresses and arrow slits."

"I like a good hard snowfight," says the old man, his knobbly fingers forming an invisible ball.

"No snowmen," says Brian shakily. (Ever since she saw a *New Yorker* magazine with a cartoon of a melting snowman on the cover, his nose falling out, Brian's been freaked out by them. How's she going to manage from January through April, Sumac wonders, when every third yard has a snowman?)

"Want a chunk of my pumpernickel pistachio bread?" asks PopCorn, offering Brian the platter.

He's been experimenting with the breadmaker, and the results are mostly horrible. Brian just sniffs at it, then pulls her head in like a turtle.

"Anybody?" asks PopCorn, looking around.

"I'm good," says Wood.

"I'm full already," says MaxiMum.

PopCorn does a theatrical toss of the head, pretending his feelings are wounded.

"Icky," says Brian.

MaxiMum gives her the look that means *manners*.

"Tell the truth," says Brian smugly, which is what the parents kept reminding her in the autumn when she was in a lying phase. (Right now she's into hitting instead.)

"Who'd like to teach us a new and interesting grace?" asks PopCorn.

"There's a Grace who sells me petrol," says Grumps.

He must be thinking of when he was still in Yukon, Sumac thinks, because in Toronto he doesn't have a car, and neither do the rest of the Lotterys.

"Should we bother with grace? We're halfway through the so-called meal," says MaxiMum.

"So-called?" Now PopCorn actually does sound hurt.

"Sorry." MaxiMum gives him a little repentant bow. "We all just want PapaDum back and cooking up a storm."

"So much!" says Sumac. "All of us Lotterys safe at home, just us again for the holidays."

"But Luiz is hilarious. What have you got against him?" demands Aspen through a mouth full of broken crackers.

"Nothing, it's only —"

Catalpa interrupts. "He is kind of irritating: too jolly, too huggy, too much."

Sumac doesn't agree. "No, it's just that I want everything back to normal."

A snort from the old Scot. "Normal, in this house? No such thing."

"Ordinary, then," Sumac tells Grumps.

"Ordinary, bored-inary," chants Aspen, pulling down her lower eyelids because she knows it makes Sumac feel sick.

"Anyway, everything will be ordinary-by-Camelottery-standards again, as of tomorrow," says PopCorn, stroking Sumac's head. (He envies her sleek black hair, especially as he has hardly any hair left himself.)

"*Camelordinary*, we could call it," suggests Aspen.

"Catalpa," says MaxiMum, "you must know a Japanese grace for before meals."

"She's Japanese?" asks Grumps puzzledly.

"No, I've just been reading a lot of manga," Catalpa tells him. "But I don't know any. . . . Or, hang on, there's *itada* something . . ." Her phone's in her hand already.

"No electronics at the table," MaxiMum reminds her.

"You *asked*," says Catalpa, tapping at the screen. "Here we go. *Itadakimasu*."

"*Itadakimasu.*" The family repeats the grace after Catalpa. Except for Grumps, who's staring into space as he often does.

"It means *I humbly receive*," says Catalpa, reading off her phone, "or *I take this nourishment in gratitude to all beings who grew, hunted, or cooked this food.*"

"Wow, that's a bunch for one word to mean," says Aspen.

"Also, BTW," Catalpa goes on, "Madison just texted about sledding this afternoon —"

"Off!" That's MaxiMum and PopCorn in unison.

Catalpa sighs, and turns her phone off. "Hey, if it gets ultra cold at the parade tonight, is there any danger my contacts will freeze?"

Catalpa's only had contact lenses since October. So far she's survived (just about) The Day She Got Mascara On A Contact, The Day She Dropped One Into A Pyramid Of Strawberries At The Farmer's Market, and The Day She Put The Left One In The Right Eye And Vice Versa And Was Horribly Dizzy Till She Figured It Out.

"It'll be an interesting experiment," says Wood in an evil-scientist voice.

MaxiMum grins. "I don't think lenses would be so popular if they froze hard."

PopCorn mimes someone walking along all carefree, la-la-la-la-la, when suddenly his eyes lock wide open.

Everyone laughs except Catalpa.

"In my day, contacts were a huge hassle," says PopCorn. "You had to take them out of your eyes at night, keep them in a cleaning solution, and put them back in the next morning, for months and months."

Catalpa makes a revolted face. "That's like reusing toilet paper!"

"One time my mom left hers in a glass and Dad drank them . . ."

Sumac joins in the howl of horror.

"What did I do?" asks Grumps.

"You swallowed her contact lenses," Sumac tells him. "Elspeth's. Your wife?"

"Nary a bit of harm it did me," insists the old man.

"There's a guy in the world record books called Monsieur Mangetout who eats two pounds of metal a day," says Wood.

"Don't get any ideas," says MaxiMum, pointing one finger at him.

Luiz is next door in the Mud Room now, whooping with laughter.

"I bet he's uploading a video of himself in the snow," says Sumac.

"What snow?" asks Grumps.

Sumac points out the window.

"Maybe the dude's Skyping his parents *again*," says Wood.

27

"What's wrong with keeping in touch?" asks PopCorn.

"But three times a day?"

"And so loudly," says Catalpa with a groan. "Who could possibly like their folks that much?"

That bothers Sumac. "Maybe when you grow up, if you're thousands of kilometers away from us," she says to Catalpa, "you'll want to talk to us sometimes."

Her sister curls her lovely lip. "Don't count on it."

MaxiMum has put her plate and cutlery in the dishwasher already. "So I wonder, should we really keep the kids outside in freezing temperatures all afternoon and evening?" she asks PopCorn.

Wood snorts. "Just wrap them up." He never feels the cold himself.

"Well," says PopCorn, "what if — instead of the Ice Sculpture Fest — we check out the flower show at the Allan Gardens Conservatory? Lovely tropical atmosphere . . ."

"We're celebrating mid*winter*," says Sumac. "We always go to the Ice Sculpture Fest and the Solstice Parade."

"What, since the dawn of time?" sneers Catalpa, clearing away her plate. "We've actually only been going for a couple of years — four, max."

"Well, that's nearly half my life," says Sumac.

"Good question, though, Cat-girl: How long does it take before something's a tradition?" asks PopCorn.

"Songs have to be donkey's years old to count as traditional music," says Catalpa. "A hundred, at least."

"My mammy lived to be ninety-four," says Grumps, sucking a fragment of cheese off his dentures.

"We're getting off the point," says Sumac.

"Before you kiddos came along, we did all sorts of different things over the winter break," PopCorn tells her. "PapaDum and I once went on a fabulous walking safari in Bali."

But Sumac thinks it's irrelevant what the adults did before the kids. The four of them weren't even Lotterys back then; they all had different surnames.

Everything began the night MaxiMum was giving birth to Sic, who they thought would be their one and only baby. CardaMom picked up a lost lottery ticket off the hospital floor to use as a bookmark. Only after Sic was safely out did the parents have a minute to check out the ticket and find (once they'd done their best to track down its owner) that they'd won enough money to give up their jobs and stay home and raise lots more kids. Everything before that, Sumac thinks of as BL: Before Lottery.

She hurries to retrieve her gigantic calendar from the cupboard under the stairs, where she left it for the glitter glue to dry. "Ta-dah! Here's what we're doing." She leans it against the freezer so everyone can read it.

29

December 21	Winter Solstice (shortest day of year!)
	Bye-bye to Luiz (our couchsurfer from Brazil)
	Ice Sculpture Fest
	Solstice Parade
December 22	PapaDum and Sic get back from Delhi in time for:
	The Nutcracker
	Saturnalia Banquet
December 23	Brian & Oak's Welcome Day
	Cut and Trim Tree
	Polar Bear Plunge *(brrr)*
December 24	Kris Kringle (made your present yet?)

December 25   The Big C!

                    Stockings

                    Dim Sum

                    Dinner

December 26   Cookie Party

Sumac thinks it looks amazing, especially the Cookie Party picture, with neighbors lining up so eagerly. (Last year, the Lotterys made eight twelve-cookie sheets of each of seven different kinds — 672 cookies! — which was enough to feed everyone on the street and send them home with full tins as well.) Also the illustration of the Polar Bear Plunge, with PopCorn and Wood bravely leaping into the icy waters of Lake Ontario. Last year, Sumac missed seeing her brother and father do the Plunge because she had a sleepover at her BFF Isabella's apartment. This time she plans to video the whole thing; it'll be the highlight of the Lotterys' home movies.

"Line up for exhausting, compulsory fun," murmurs Catalpa.

Sumac looks daggers at her big sister.

"Who's getting cancer on the twenty-fifth?" asks Wood. "Huh?"

Her brother points at the calendar. *The Big C!*

"I meant Christmas," says Sumac, her whole face heating up. She takes a permanent marker and adds *hristmas Day* to *The Big C*, but you can still tell the *h* used to be an exclamation point.

Grumps is studying the list, head tilted to one side. "Have I met Dim Sum?"

Aspen laughs. "It's lots of different Chinese foods."

"We always go out for dim sum with Baruch and Ben and their crew," Catalpa tells their grandfather.

He squints at the date. "On Christmas?"

"It's a Jewish thing."

"Oh, aye," says Grumps in his you-can't-fool-me voice.

"Let's cut a few boring things, like *The Nutcracker*," suggests Aspen. "We could make up some new festivities. Like, what about twenty-four hours of Minecraft? I wonder if we'd start to see cubed . . ."

"None of these are *boring*," says Sumac, rapping on the calendar. "Anyway, it's like turkey for Christmas dinner: traditional."

"The dullest of meats, in my opinion," murmurs PopCorn.

"Very dry," says Grumps, nodding.

"We always have turkey and it's delicious!" Sumac feels especially let down by Grumps: Shouldn't you be able to rely on a man of eighty-three to like things to stay the way they are?

"Sweetheart, you could be just a little flexible," suggests PopCorn in his I-used-to-be-a-counselor voice. "Like, sure, we'll go see *The Nutcracker*, but maybe a modern version this year?"

But the ballet's from the nineteenth century. "Modern how?" asks Sumac.

He holds up the city freesheet that lists pages and pages of events. "Look, there's a jazz one with the men wearing motion-sensor lights on their tutus."

Sumac scrunches up her nose. "We have our tickets already." Then, "Don't we?"

"Ah," says PopCorn doubtfully. "It's PapaDum who usually sees to that stuff . . ."

MaxiMum gets up to examine the pieces of paper held on to the refrigerators by magnet dolls of Albert Einstein and Sojourner Truth, Frida Kahlo and Mahatma Gandhi. "No sign of them. Grrr." (Which, from somebody so calm, is like steam coming out of MaxiMum's ears.)

"Very dry meat," says Grumps again.

"Oh well, let's take our chances and pop along to this jazz *Nutcracker* tomorrow," says PopCorn. "Who says aye aye?"

Sumac sighs. Her dad prides himself on being spontaneous and seizing the day, so he's always suggesting the Lotterys *nip along, have a bash, wing it,* or *cross their fingers.* . . . In her experience, there won't be any tickets left. Well, at least that means she won't have to see the motion-sensor tutus.

And then the front door scrapes open and CardaMom rushes in with Oak riding on her shoulders. "*Kwe,* everybody!" That's *hi* in Mohawk. "We're famished!"

Sumac jumps up to be the first to hug her baby brother, even if his pirate bandana bib is all drooly.

CHAPTER 2

- - - - - - - - - - - - - - - - - - - -
PARADING

In the afternoon, Sumac's been ready to go and standing in the Hall of Mirrors for ages. (She always keeps her gloves, hats, and scarves hidden in her bedroom in the attic, so

they won't get grabbed by some flakey sibling who's dropped their own at the park.) She's pleased with her costume: silver-sprayed paper snowflakes hot-glued all over an old white sundress of CardaMom's, on top of layers of thermals.

Aspen clunks down the stairs in her Rollerblades.

"Horrible!" says Sumac.

Aspen bows, accepting it as a compliment. "I'm Santa's demon accomplice, Krampus." She slurs because of the fake fangs, and lets her tongue loll out; she's dyed it with something really red. "I'm demonically charming, heh heh heh! Except when I stuff naughty kids in my sack."

MaxiMum comes out of the Mess. She refuses to dress up ever, so she's in her regular long coat.

"Won't you feel out of place at the Solstice Parade?" asks Sumac.

MaxiMum grins. "I was born feeling out of place. It doesn't bother me." Turning to Aspen, she asks, "Blades off, please: It's slippy and blowy out there."

"Nah, I'll just hold on to people." Aspen grips Sumac's shoulder painfully and zooms right around her, her broom almost knocking a mirror off the wall.

"Nah, pickney," says MaxiMum, "you'll put your boots on." (Pickney's what they call a little kid in Jamaica, where MaxiMum was born.)

PopCorn comes downstairs covered with bits of leather and fake fur, with Oak tucked horizontally under his arm, in a fleecy orange starfish costume, with the fifth arm pointing up from his head: adorable! Oak's squeezing a banana in his fist. Sumac rescues it, breaks it in two, and gives him back one half.

"Ba!" says Oak.

"That's right, ba-na-na. Oaky-doke likes bananas." Sumac's surprised Luiz didn't get to this one first. "Is Luiz coming?"

"Not to the ice sculptures," says MaxiMum. "I've persuaded Catalpa to take him sledding with her friends before it turns to rain and washes away all the snow."

Brian stomps up from the basement in armor and a horned helmet, brandishing an axe. Sumac's explained to her that Vikings didn't actually wear horns, but Brian pays no attention.

"Do you think maybe you don't need the earmuffs as well as the helmet?" Sumac asks her.

"Poor horns be cold," says Brian, stroking them.

"That wind's really picking up," mentions MaxiMum, watching branches whip outside the semicircular window over the door.

"Aha!" PopCorn uses a dry-erase marker to add his latest quote to a mirror.

Sumac reads over his shoulder. "You can't . . . control the wine?"

"Well, that's true," says MaxiMum, laughing.

"The *wind*." PopCorn tidies up the *d. "You can't control the wind, but you can trim your sails." Anon*, he puts, which means nobody knows who first said it.

"Your scribble's worse than any of ours except Brian's," Sumac tells PopCorn. She feels a hard blow on the back of her leg. "Ow!"

That was Brian's foam axe.

PopCorn squats beside Brian. "Gentle hands if you want to go to the parade."

"Not hands," says Brian, lower lip stuck out. "Axe."

CardaMom runs downstairs in that dress she never usually wears because it's *too* yellow.

"What are you supposed to be?" asks Sumac.

"The sun, of course." She hurries them up: "*Oksa, oksa,* everyone, let's hustle!"

Wood appears in a hoodie and shorts, with Diamond at his side.

"You know people sometimes scold us for letting you out without a coat in midwinter?" PopCorn asks him.

Wood shrugs. "What do you care what *people* say?"

"Well, he hasn't gotten hypothermia yet," MaxiMum points out, "so can we go?"

"Here, you could carry the water drum," CardaMom suggests, "just to get in the parade spirit." She hands it to Wood with a slosh. Their baba (CardaMom's dad) made it out of birch wood and moose hide. "Are we still missing somebody?"

"Dad?" calls PopCorn.

Emerging from the Grumpery, their grandfather bends over to give their three-legged mongrel a good hard pat along her spine. Grumps has a tricorn hat on top of his everyday jeans and old winter jacket.

"Who are you, a pirate?" Sumac asks him.

"Napoleon," Brian corrects her. That's what she calls all the people who lived a long time ago: Napoleons.

"All the same to me, hen," says Grumps with a shrug.

MaxiMum spots that he still has his slippers on, and it takes a while to persuade the old man that they aren't grippy enough for snowy streets.

Sumac picks up her lantern and fits it onto its bamboo pole . . .

But then CardaMom's mislaid her wallet, and Sumac gets "volunteered" to run up to the moms' room, where she finds it under a jumble of open books.

Then Slate sticks his head out of Aspen's cloak.

The parents got the rat from a rodent rescue shelter specially for Aspen because having a pet of her own was supposed to make her more calm and responsible. (Ha!) Sumac doesn't find Slate creepy anymore — and he smells quite nice, like warm taco chips — but he's not allowed in public places, especially since the Great Movie Theater Disaster. Right now Aspen's arguing that Slate's a crucial piece of her Krampus costume . . . but the parents make her go put him back in the nine-level deluxe cage she got for her birthday.

Now they're *finally* out the door. The icy, wet wind makes Sumac's eyes water. Diamond trots along the street, sniffing at everything, on guard.

"Look," says MaxiMum to Brian, pointing out a Finnish flag. "The wind's trying to make the flag go sideways, but gravity says to hang straight down."

"Wind not listening to Gabbity," says Brian.

"It's *gravity*," Sumac corrects her.

"Gabbity!"

There's no point arguing. So Sumac says, "Come on, Wind, you can do it. Push the flag sideways."

Brian puts her fists up like a tiny boxer. "Come on, Gabbity, downways!"

A drop down the back of her neck makes Sumac flinch.

Wood reads from his phone in an I-told-you-so tone: *"Freezing rain . . . caused by a warm front sandwiched between a cold air mass high up and another shallow layer of cold air at ground level."*

Sumac wonders where the warm air is in the sandwich, because she can't feel any, just shuddery damp. She pulls out *Little Women* to distract herself. (She never goes out without three paperbacks in her backpack.)

"Who thinks it's a smart idea to read while walking down a busy street?" CardaMom wonders aloud.

"I'm using my what-do-you-call-it, my peripheral vision," Sumac answers, her eyes still on the page. The Lotterys aren't even moving that fast, because Brian insists on walking instead of riding on her board at the back of Oak's stroller.

"Mm, I remember doing that once," said CardaMom, "and I walked smack into a utility pole. See this scar?"

That makes Sumac stop, look up, and finger her mother's forehead till she finds the tiny line nearly hidden in one eyebrow. Huh, a family story Sumac didn't know. "Yeah, but I'm way more present-minded than you," she points out, "so I can manage both things at once."

Present-minded is a handy word Aspen made up to describe people like Sumac who aren't absentminded like Aspen is.

CardaMom grins. "Best of luck with that, *tsi't-ha*." (That's something Mohawk people call birds, or sometimes their kids.)

Sumac reads on, until two drops of freezing rain splash on the page.

"We always stop at the I Scream on the way to the Ice Sculpture Fest," she reminds the family as they come up to it.

In winter there's no line, because most people don't think of buying ice cream when it's cold. But actually, a fun fact Sumac knows is that the fat in the ice cream warms you up.

"Look at you guys!" The server shakes his head at their costumes, whether impressed, or embarrassed for the Lotterys, it's hard for Sumac to tell.

"We're parading. Going to the Solstice Parade," she explains.

"The one where they set stuff on fire at the end?"

She nods. "I've never stayed late enough to see the burning bit before, but this year I'm allowed to because I'm nearly ten."

"Cool."

You're allowed two taster spoons, so Sumac tries chocolate and bacon (disgusting) and lavender ginger (so-so). What she actually orders is Yule spice, because it sounds festive.

Brian's taken off her helmet and earmuffs to scratch her buzz-cut head, and the server's offering "as many tasters as you like, buddy." He's got that sappy look that means he thinks this brave little boy's hair has all fallen out because of cancer treatment. When in fact the worst thing Brian's ever had is pink eye.

Brian orders Madagascan vanilla to be the same as Oak, even though they all know she'd actually prefer berry mashup if she could persuade her little brother to like it instead of spitting it all down himself. She gets an extra sprinkle of mini marshmallows on hers, as her reward for not hitting anyone since they left the house.

"Though the day's not over yet," murmurs MaxiMum, "so it seems a bit early for a reward."

"Brian," says PopCorn, "eating the marshmallows means you hundred-percent-promise not to hit anyone, all the way till bed-time, right?"

Brian nods and swallows a huge spoonful of vanilla.

Oak smears his ice cream down his right cheek, then his left.

"And marshmallows for Oaky?" suggests Brian.

"Well . . ." PopCorn dithers, unable to decide.

"He don't hit people too," Brian points out.

"You make a strong case," MaxiMum tells her, "but —"

"What about me?" That's Aspen interrupting, outraged. "I hardly ever hit anybody."

43

"But you're a lot older than Brian," mutters Sumac, "and you do hurt us by accident, all the time, like yesterday, when you were playing Frisbee in the Loud Lounge."

"Oh, what the heck, mini marshmallows all around," cries PopCorn generously.

"Not *fair*," roars Brian, lifting her axe and whapping him on the back of the head.

So MaxiMum confiscates Brian's ice cream and hands it back to the server . . .

"Hang on," CardaMom protests. "Sharing Brian's marshmallow reward with everybody really wasn't fair."

So PopCorn has to apologize to Brian and ask the server for the vanilla back . . . but by now it's in the garbage. So he pays for another, with more marshmallows.

"That's rewarding a tantrum *and* a blow to the head," says MaxiMum. "At the very least Brian's axe has to be put away." So she tucks it in the bag behind Oak's stroller . . .

And Brian bites her on the arm. Her teeth leave a mark, right through the sleeve of MaxiMum's coat!

When the Lotterys are all outside, wiping ice cream off faces (and trying to scrub it out of Oak's costume), and the screams have lulled, MaxiMum says, "Maybe I'll just take the smalls home."

"*Not* home," howls Brian.

"That wouldn't be fair, if you got bitten *and* had to miss the parade," CardaMom tells MaxiMum, stroking her sore arm.

"Oh, believe me, hon, I'm not really in the mood anymore."

"Come on, pax, everybody?" PopCorn's voice is pleading, with a little sob in it. "Let's all go, it'll be fab."

So the Lotterys chorus "Pax." (Even Brian, who's still broodily eyeing the handle of the axe protruding from MaxiMum's backpack.)

The first two streetcars are full, and the parents don't want to split up the family, so they wait for the next. Aspen cracks every one of her knuckles.

"Stop that," orders Sumac.

"You're going to wear out your joints," MaxiMum tells Aspen.

"Remember, sweetie, it causes arthritis later in life," PopCorn adds.

Aspen cracks three more knuckles.

To pass the time, CardaMom tells them a legend about a Mohawk boy called Three Arrows who discovered how to make fire for his people. She gets Brian and Sumac to be the two balsam twigs, and Aspen the boy rubbing them together.

Finally a half-empty streetcar arrives.

Sumac takes a seat beside PopCorn. "If PapaDum was home from Delhi already," she says, "we'd have made our cabbage rolls this morning."

Last year Sumac and her friend Isabella were PapaDum's co-chefs in tall paper hats, helping him cook thirty kilos of cabbage. (Isabella's away too at the moment — her family's gone back to Colombia for the whole holidays.)

PopCorn sighs and, for once, says nothing.

He's probably just as stressed out as MaxiMum by PapaDum not being home for the holidays yet, Sumac realizes. The parents are like a relay team missing one of their four members, and trying not to drop the baton. Sumac should be like some super-speedy kid who runs in and picks up the baton and saves the day.

Aspen leans over the back of her seat to tell Sumac, "You're parentsick. Like, homesick but for a parent."

"And I know PapaDum's feeling *child*sick for you," PopCorn tells Sumac.

"Of course, we need a word for sometimes being sick *of* parents too," says Aspen, dropping back into her seat.

The sun's setting already and it's not even a quarter to five. "Our stop!" Aspen shrieks, and the Lotterys push forward through the crowded streetcar. They almost leave Grumps behind, but Wood and Diamond run back for him.

It's twilight by the time they reach the Ice Sculpture

Fest, but there are floodlights to show off the carvings. Some are the best Sumac's ever seen: an angel, a centaur (half man, half horse), a Santa Claus, and a twice-life-sized Michael Jackson. She takes photos from underneath to make them look even more dramatic. She finds a turkey, a peacock, a moose, Olaf and Elsa from *Frozen*, a creeper from Minecraft . . . and there's even a sculpture of a woman with a chisel sculpting a block of ice into a smaller sculpture of a woman sculpting a tiny block of ice into a smaller sculpture . . . and on and on. "This one's the very best," she tells PopCorn, peering at it to see where the last little chiseling woman becomes a blur.

"Definitely the most original," says PopCorn. "Not *traditional* at all, is it?"

Sumac purses her lips, because she can tell he's making a point.

CardaMom hurries up, wiping rain off her face. "We'd better head for the parade, because if the weather gets worse MaxiMum's going to take the smalls home."

"Nine doesn't count as a small, by the way," says Sumac. "I'm a middle, and I'm staying till the big fire at the end."

Brian insists on holding her see-through umbrella over her brother in his stroller, to keep the icy drizzle off him. Oak starts to thrash with excitement as they get within earshot of the first band. He plants his heels on the rubber strip at the bottom of his stroller and tries to stand up, but the straps frustrate him.

"You dancing, Oaky?" Brian asks him. "Dance?"

"Da!"

So many lanterns, bobbing by in the dark like luminous fish — lots of them much more artistic than Sumac's moon one, she has to admit. Flaming torches and nine-lamp menorahs. Signs saying *Light Up the Longest Night*, and *Ignite the Dark*. Clowns with powdered faces (streaky from the rain) and red noses, buzzing on kazoos. Dancers in pointed hats and cloaks. Dogs in skirts with LED crowns.

Sumac starts filming with the night setting on: kind of blurry, but in an atmospheric way. (CardaMom's set her the challenge of learning to edit video, so Sumac's in charge of the Lotterys' Highlights Reel this year, and she's going to make sure the holiday sequence is the best ever.)

There's a saxophone quintet playing a cheerful, stomping version of "I Saw the Light," a band of masked and feathered drummers farther down the street, and a ukulele group in wings with a banner that says they're called Entertaining Angels.

"Put the tablet away and dance," CardaMom shouts in her ear, so Sumac does. At the Solstice Parade, there's no audience: Everyone's taking part, moving through

the streets. The drums make her heart boom, and the saxophones get her butt shaking. As Sumac waves her lantern pole from side to side, like she's fishing in the freezing, wet air, she's starting to catch the holiday feeling at last.

Grumps gawks in all directions as if he's found himself on another planet. He's only wearing one glove. Sumac takes his long, bare fingers in her wooly ones.

"Circus, is it?" he asks.

"Ah . . . more or less," she tells him.

Wood's beside them, with Diamond, who's so level-headed, she doesn't turn a hair even in the oddest of situations. "Maybe we should have made her a costume?" asks Sumac, thinking how cute that would have looked in the home video — but her brother doesn't hear over the cacophony of music.

A papier-mâché sailboat goes by, and a multiarmed sea creature. Anishinaabe kids are doing complicated dances with luminous hoops that they make into tails and wings and globes. A man with a massive beard hands Sumac a can filled with — it sounds like — dry beans. Wood is making surprisingly good beats on the water drum. There's a man on stilts wearing a sun mask.

Sumac's eyeing the food trucks: Maybe for dinner they could have those deep-fried Japanese hot dogs on purple rice? The rain's getting heavier and the road slippier but she's not, not, not going to go home early with Brian and Oak.

PopCorn bends to speak to Sumac, his fake fur tickling her face. "You know who I first laid eyes on at the very first of these parades, twenty-five years ago?"

"PapaDum!"

"You're the keeper of the stories," he says with a grin. "Of course, he was called Manraj then. I didn't know we'd end up having seven kids together."

Something terrible occurs to Sumac. "But that means PapaDum's missing the quarter-century anniversary of the night you met!"

"Ah, don't worry, patoot, he's getting on the plane to come home any minute. Or has he already, if it's Sunday in India?" asks PopCorn puzzledly.

Here's Catalpa, waving from across the street. She ducks under a giant bird puppet to run over to her family. She's not in costume, just black droopy things as usual. She and her friends have drawn curly lines all over each other's faces with eyeliner. It looks like that mehndi tattoo Sumac got on her wrist at the mosque's Open Day.

"How did you like sledding, Luiz?" shouts PopCorn.

"Very, very." Luiz does a double thumbs-up. He's all buddyish with the teenagers; they're putting glow sticks through his curls. (It occurs to Sumac that even though

Catalpa finds Luiz annoying, she's enjoying giving her friends the impression she hangs out with nearly-twenty-year-old world travelers.)

"What hill did they take you to?" asks CardaMom.

Luiz shakes his head: "No hill. I am good to flop now."

Flopping's when you run along behind a moving sled and jump on.

"I do it before many times, but no snow. In my favela where I am living in Rio, sometimes we slide down the grass on the plastic bags," he explains, his hand making a steep slope.

Wow. That sounds painful.

"I have many, many new English today," Luiz goes on, "like the *wipe*."

"Wipeout," says Catalpa, correcting him in a teacherly tone.

"Yeah, when I totally fall in the snow, that I love!"

Now Luiz is sambaing beside Sumac. He sticks his phone out to take an ussie.

He's an excellent dancer — which makes sense, because Rio has the biggest carnival in the world. "Did you have a good last afternoon in Canada?" she shouts.

Double thumbs-up. "Only now I have the bad eye."

Sumac wonders if that's some strange expression for a hangover.

He rubs his right eye. "Fireworks."

"Where are they?" Sumac spins around, thrilled.

"In my head. Flash flash!" Luiz mimes explosions, half laughing.

Catalpa and her giggling friend Feng butt in, telling Luiz some complicated plot of a manga series, so Sumac can't ask him anything more.

Suddenly she feels very cold and wet. Also worried. She edges through the crowd to the nearest parent: MaxiMum, having her nightly cigarette against a taco van and holding an umbrella over their sleeping orange starfish.

Sumac starts cautiously. "I'm not sure Luiz should get his bus to the airport."

"Worried he'll be late?" asks MaxiMum. "Should we call him a cab?"

"I'm actually not sure he should be going anywhere at all right now."

MaxiMum looks at Sumac levelly.

"I don't want to tattle, but it might be a life-or-death situation."

"Like the other evening, when you came downstairs to report that Wood was tapping the egg timer to make his two minutes of toothbrushing go faster?"

Sumac squirms. "Well . . . can't people die of gum disease?"

MaxiMum winks without moving anything but her eyelid. (Whenever Sumac tries, half her face scrunches.) "Tapping doesn't make the sand go through faster."

Sumac frowns. "Doesn't it, really?"

"So let your brother tap, if it gives him an illusory sense of power."

She grins. "OK."

"You're wonderfully reliable, especially for a nine-year-old," MaxiMum tells her, "but sometimes . . ."

"I'm a worrywart." Then Sumac remembers her mission. "Right now it really probably is life or death, though, because Luiz may be on some scary drugs."

"What makes you think so?" asks MaxiMum, calm as ever.

"He says one of his eyes is heavy, with fireworks going off in his head."

MaxiMum blinks at her. Then pulls out her phone, rather fast, and starts one-finger typing.

CHAPTER 3

- - - - - - - - - - - - - - - - - - - -

THE LONGEST NIGHT

The Lotterys (or four of the female ones, anyway) are in the waiting room of the emergency department. When MaxiMum rounded them all up in the hullabaloo of the parade and told them that Luiz seemed to have injured his eye, CardaMom volunteered to take him to the hospital. Catalpa's come along too, of course, because she's the one who brought their guest sledding, and when he hit his head on a tree stump she *never even thought to mention it!* Aspen decided to tag along for the novelty of not being the patient this time. (She's had so many accidents, the Lotterys call them her *aspendents*.) And Sumac's here because she feels bad about having assumed Luiz was on drugs.

Right now Catalpa's glumly removing the eyeliner drawings from her face with a makeup wipe, and Luiz is squinting at his phone.

"Shut your eyes and rest them, you poor boy," says CardaMom. She's on her feet as usual, hovering by the plastic chairs, because she doesn't much like sitting, especially if she's worried.

"I just wonder is my plane gone yet," he says, tapping the screen.

"Sorry, you're not getting on any plane tonight," CardaMom tells him. "You could have a concussion."

Catalpa lets out a guilty groan and scrubs at her neck with the wipe.

"I could test how his brains are working," Sumac suggests. "Luiz, what's the square root of one hundred and sixty-nine?"

"I don't guess what you mean," he says.

"Leave him alone, freakazoid," says Aspen, with a glare at Sumac.

"You know many mathematics," Luiz says to Sumac admiringly. "Your school has the holidays for lots of days now, on Christmas?"

"Oh, we don't get holidays," Aspen tells him tragically.

"*Como assim?*" He doesn't understand.

"We don't go to school," says Sumac, "so it's kind of like we're on vacation all year."

"No it's not," says Aspen, "it's like school at home every day of the year, with the four boringest teachers."

CardaMom laughs at that.

Luiz looks puzzled. "The schools in Canada, you have to pay?"

CardaMom shakes her head.

"But — excuse, I don't understand — your kids, they don't go?"

Sumac tries to explain. "We learn by doing."

"And by making mistakes," says Aspen enthusiastically.

"Going on Out-and-Aboutings, and talking to strangers," adds Sumac. "Though sometimes we ask so many questions, they think we're nosy creeps."

Aspen clicks her fingers, remembering something. "We set the bucket on fire."

That really makes Luiz stare.

CardaMom laughs again. "She means — there's a quote we read somewhere — *education's not the filling of a bucket, it's the lighting of a fire.*"

Luiz beckons to Sumac with his finger, and she leans down to him. He murmurs in her ear, "I am wonder, the hospitals they are free too, like the schools?"

She tries to remember a learning day the Lotterys had on All the Great Stuff Our Taxes Pay For. "Well, free if you live here," she whispers. "I guess if you're visiting, you use your insurance?"

Luiz bites his lip like it's meat.

"Travel insurance?" Sumac repeats. "For emergencies when you're away from home?"

He wrinkles his nose. "Too much price."

"*Eye*-mergencies," says Aspen. "Get it? Eye-mergencies!"

"Araújo," says a nurse. Then he repeats it, more loudly: "Luiz Araújo?"

"Is that you?" Sumac asks Luiz.

The nurse leads him off to be examined.

Now the four Lotterys are alone, CardaMom turns on Catalpa. "So tell me how it happened. I assume Luiz had a helmet on?"

Catalpa's face twists. "Well . . . we'd have lent him one of ours, and taken turns, but he said he was cool without one."

"Cool without one?"

Her big sister's squirming so much under their mother's gaze, Sumac's almost sorry for her. "OK OK OK," says Catalpa with a gulp, "I messed up. I should have told him you *have* to wear a helmet for sledding. And I didn't realize

the rain — it was making this sort of glaze — everything was so incredibly slippery . . ."

CardaMom paces up and down the waiting room.

"What's my punishment?" Catalpa wants to know.

"We don't punish," says CardaMom, as if the word tastes bad.

"Yeah, you guys do," says Catalpa, "you just call it *consequences*. What do I have to do?"

CardaMom's mouth presses shut. "I'm sure we'll think of something."

Sumac finds herself staring at a woman nearby with one leg swollen to twice the thickness of the other. She makes herself look away. There's a teenager with red-stained bandages all up his arms. Behind him, an oldish guy with a smashed face. Maybe Sumac should cross *doctor* off her list of possible jobs.

CardaMom suddenly marches past the nurses' station calling, "Luiz?"

A distant cry: "Am here, *amigas*!"

The three girls hurry off after their mom.

"Immediate family only, please," says the doctor, as the Lotterys crowd in behind the curtain.

Luiz is flat on the bed, staring at the ceiling tiles.

Sumac starts to back out again, but Catalpa blocks

her. "We're like his family at the moment," she tells the doctor.

Doctor Yazdani — that's what it says on the badge pinned to the bottom of her hijab — briefly stares at their costumes, then looks back at Luiz. "As I was telling Mr. Araújo, he's suffered a retinal detachment, which is particularly common in young men."

"*Aki!*" CardaMom sucks in her breath sympathetically. "That must hurt, Luiz. Basically a bit of the back of your eye's come loose."

He groans.

"Could you turn that off, please?" asks the doctor, pointing at the tablet that Aspen's using to video the drama. She tells Luiz, "The blow to your head has caused a small superior flap tear in the retina of your right eye."

Superior, like *superior nutrition for your pet*? "Does *superior* mean it's a good kind to have?" Sumac asks the doctor.

Doctor Yazdani shakes her head tiredly. (Some adults find Sumac's eager-to-learn attitude charming. Others, not so much.) "*Superior*, as in the *upper* rear section, at eleven o'clock." She points up and a little to the left.

That's funny, Sumac thinks: like the eye is a ticking clock.

"Fluid is now leaking under your retina," the doctor tells

Luiz, "and peeling it away. Like wallpaper — do you understand?"

"Ew," cries Aspen.

Luiz nods fearfully.

"Now, you have a good chance of ultimately recovering full vision," says Doctor Yazdani.

Luiz lets out his breath noisily, like a relieved whale.

"*Ultimately*," CardaMom repeats to him, squeezing his shoulder, "which means not right away."

"How many of days, please?" Luiz asks.

"First things first," says Doctor Yazdani. "You need a procedure called pneumatic retinopexy. I'll seal the rip in your eyeball with a laser, and inject an air bubble inside to keep the rip pressed shut."

Sumac has never heard anything more repulsive in her life.

Doctor Yazdani goes on, "It can be done by local anesthetic —"

"That means you'll be awake for it," CardaMom tells Luiz brightly.

He looks as if he'd really rather not.

"— but it will only work if you're compliant — that means follow the rules," the doctor warns. "You'll need to posture for the first week: stay sitting upright, leaning forward, to keep the air bubble in place."

"The first *week*?" says Catalpa, incredulous.

"Five days at the very least," says Doctor Yazdani.

Luiz's head lifts off the pillow.

"Until your procedure, please stay lying down," she tells him, "or gravity will worsen the peeling."

Luiz tries to sit up again, with a nervous smile. "I think I go now for my plane. Thank you, Doctor, I get better super soon."

"Not without surgery, you won't. You'll go blind in your right eye."

Luiz's mouth falls open and he lies back down.

"That's better. Enjoy lying on your back for the last time this week," says Doctor Yazdani, with a flicker of a smile, as she starts tapping something into the computer.

Sumac tugs at the long sleeve of the very yellow dress till CardaMom bends down. Does this count as tattling again? But Luiz never said it was a secret. "He doesn't have insurance," she whispers.

"Ah! I should have thought." CardaMom straightens up. "Luiz, by the way, don't worry about the cost of the treatment. We broke it, we'll fix it."

Relief goes across his face like a wave. *"Obrigado,"* he says — which must mean thanks, Sumac decides. He shuts his eyes.

"Busy night, Doctor?" CardaMom asks.

Doctor Yazdani nods, covering a yawn with her hand. "Careless drivers, on highways coated with ice. . . . And it's only going to get worse."

Aspen cracks her knuckles particularly loudly.

"Stop that," barks Catalpa. "You're giving yourself arthritis."

"Actually," says the doctor, "there's no conclusive evidence in the medical literature that knuckle cracking has harmful effects."

Sumac can't believe that.

"Score!" Aspen lifts a fist in triumph.

"Other than annoying other people, of course," mutters Doctor Yazdani on her way out of the cubicle.

"Double score!" Aspen's two fists are held high.

The Lotterys wait with Luiz behind the curtain for what feels like hours. Sumac's stomach growls; is it disloyal to their couchsurfer to think about getting snacks from the vending machine? "Poor you," she tells Luiz. "Getting hurt *and* missing your flight *and* having to spend Christmas in the hospital too." Maybe the Lotterys could visit him if they've got time?

Catalpa makes a faint snort. "He's not spending it in the hospital."

Sumac's confused. "Where's he spending it, then?"

"Paris," says Aspen confidently.

64

"Camelottery, of course," CardaMom corrects her.

"*Local* anesthetic, that means numbing just his eyeball," Catalpa tells her younger sisters in a flat voice, "so he'll come home with us right afterward."

"*Desculpe*," says Luiz. "I will search another couch for the surf."

"Don't be ridiculous," says CardaMom. "Stay with us and we'll look after you, Luiz. The more the merrier!"

That's not always true, in Sumac's experience; sometimes her family is too much *more* already, and it's *the more the crankier*. The thing about a wise old saying is, there's nearly always another wise old saying that contradicts it. Like *many hands make light work*, but *too many cooks spoil the broth*.

She wonders if Luiz is worrying about the air bubble operation. Sumac would be. How can she distract him? "I was born right here in this hospital," she tells him.

"Ah, yeah? And you are her *mamãe*, right?" Luiz asks, looking toward CardaMom.

"Huh?" says Sumac.

CardaMom smiles down at him. "Which of us is Sumac's mom, me or MaxiMum, is that what you're asking?"

Aspen butts in: "Both of them — but also, neither, like, DNA-ishly."

"I didn't come out of either of their bodies," Sumac explains. Though she sees how Luiz might have assumed it was CardaMom, because Sumac's Filipina and German genes and CardaMom's Mohawk ones happen to have given them similar wide faces and straight black hair. When Sumac's on her own, or with any of the three parents she looks nothing like, people read her as anything from Mexican to Maori to Greek.

Luiz is looking really confused now, so Sumac tells him the whole story. "See, my birth parents are called Nenita and Jensen, and they gave me to my dads and moms as soon as I was born."

He nods sympathetically. "They're super poor, this Nenita and Jensen?"

Sumac frowns, not following. "I don't think so; they're accountants. They just didn't want to be parents, and CardaMom and MaxiMum and PopCorn and PapaDum really, really did."

"*Compreendo*, I get it. One more question, Mrs. Lottery —"

"I'm Mary, or Wari in Mohawk," says CardaMom, "though the family call me CardaMom."

"If you're staying five more days, we'd better teach you our names," Sumac tells him.

"I wonder, excuse my curious," he asks CardaMom, "which is your husband? The *papai* who is brown like me, or the pale one?"

He means PapaDum and PopCorn, thinks Sumac.

Aspen cackles, way too loud.

"Oh dear, we really didn't do proper introductions, Luiz, did we?" says CardaMom with a laugh. "You must have arrived on a busy day."

But that describes pretty much every day at Camelottery, Sumac thinks. That's what it's like in a family of twelve.

Catalpa speaks up without lifting her eyes from her phone. "The moms are a couple, and so are the dads, right? Like, gay?"

"Ah!" Luiz's face clears. "Sorry, now *compreendo*."

Sumac's yawning, like the doctor. Not surprising, really, because it's after ten o'clock. She takes out her *Greek Myths: The Graphic Novel* to keep herself awake, and reads a freaky one about a king called Nisus with a strand of purple hair that makes him invincible.

CardaMom goes off in search of the washroom. Catalpa leans against the wall checking her phone, looking — Sumac thinks — as cool and lovely as a girl in a movie. Aspen isn't sleepy — as usual. She roams around, peeking at medical supplies.

"Don't touch," Sumac reminds her. She goes back to her book and is horrified to discover that the king's daughter, Scylla, is about to cut his purple hair off . . .

Then it occurs to her she should be talking to the patient to keep his mind off his eyeball. "Luiz, why do you like bananas so much?"

"I don't very," says Luiz.

That startles Sumac. "How come you're always eating ours, then?" That came out rude. "Sorry, I just mean, you seem to eat them a lot."

"When I first come to travel, in summertime, I miss my fruits so much, you know, like —" Luiz stiffens and twitches.

"You had a fit?" asks Aspen.

"Like someone who need the drug *bad*," he explains. "In Brazil, it's açaí, mamão, you know?"

Sumac's never heard of those.

"Or goiaba," Luiz goes on, "or guaraná that wake us up like coffee but double, manga . . ."

Sumac thought that meant comics. "Can't you find them here in supermarkets?" she asks.

Luiz's fingers make the rubbing gesture that means money. "My juicy fruits cost much. So I eat bananas because nothing better."

"They're better than nothing?" asks Sumac.

"Yeah yeah."

How weird. Sumac tries to imagine going off around the world when she's nineteen, and desperately missing something like bread, and having to make do with something like couscous or cassava that doesn't taste anything like it. "Hey, I have a fruit joke for you," she tells him.

"Yes?" he says.

"Don't," Aspen begs Sumac.

Sumac ignores her sister. "So, Luiz: What do you have when you have seven oranges in one hand, and five in the other?" Was that clear enough? "Like, say, seven oranges in your right hand, and five in your left hand."

Catalpa covers her eyes as if she's embarrassed to be related to Sumac.

"Twelve oranges," says Luiz, triumphant.

"No, but hang on — picture it." Sumac spreads her fingers to grip the imaginary oranges.

Luiz does the same.

"What do you have?" she asks again.

Aspen's pretending to bang her head on the medical supplies cabinet.

"I don't know what," admits Luiz, still grinning, "only the oranges."

So Sumac delivers the punch line. "Big hands!"

The silence stretches.

69

"Your hands must be big if you can hold that many oranges, see?" she explains to Luiz.

He nods.

"That was the joke," she adds in a small voice.

"Aha, right," says Luiz, clicking his fingers. "Extra funny!"

Sumac is still crushed, but she appreciates his kindness.

Aspen's swiped two blue gloves from the doctor's box and is blowing them up into scary balloons. "Now *here* are some big hands."

"In Brazil, we have many fruit things we say. If I mean . . ." Luiz seems to be struggling to find an alternative for something really rude. "Please go away now? We say, *Go to pick coconuts!*"

"That's cool." Catalpa looks up from her phone. "Your retina probably detached because you have a long eyeball."

"He does not," objects Sumac.

"Aspen, stop that!" CardaMom comes back into the cubicle and snatches the box of blue gloves away from her.

Aspen hides her real hands in her sleeves and holds the balloon hands in the cuffs instead. She flaps them horribly: "Beware of Bulgy Finger Monster!"

It's actually a bit funny, Sumac has to admit.

"Ever notice how thick Luiz's glasses are?" Catalpa goes on. "That means he's really shortsighted because his

70

eyeball is extra long, so his retina's stretched like plastic wrap and it's more likely to tear. He could have done it *by sneezing or coughing or just bending over,*" she reads from her phone.

"Except that this happened because you took him sledding without a helmet," CardaMom points out in a steely voice, sounding like the lawyer she used to be. "I can't believe you're trying to blame the victim."

"I am no the victim," says Luiz, lifting his head. "I like to thrill-seek —"

"Me too, *amigo.* YOLO!" That's Aspen, offering him a high five.

Luiz slaps her palm, but limply.

"We've got four uncles on our family's reserve, and they're massive thrill-seekers," Aspen boasts. "One of them fell off the roof of a barn, and now he has a metal rod in his leg. And hey, if you could have hurt your eye just by sneezing, isn't it cool you did it a fun way instead?"

"No, I don't think that's the lesson here," snaps CardaMom.

"*Por favor,* no fighting."

"We're not fighting, Luiz, we're discussing —"

"Please, is my fault," he wails. "I let go."

That puzzles Sumac. "When?"

"I let go and I fall," Luiz admits, "that's the why."

"You let go of what, the sled?" asks CardaMom.

"No, the how do you call it, the bit of the car, so I fall down on the street and slide and hit the — the bump of the tree."

"*A:keh!*" CardaMom's voice goes very high. "You were holding on to a car?"

Catalpa's got her hands up, hiding nearly her whole face.

Their mother turns on her. "Don't tell me you took him *skitching*!"

When parents say *don't tell me*, strangely enough, what they actually mean is *tell me right this minute*. "What's skitching?" asks Sumac.

"It was Feng's idea," says Catalpa weakly.

"I don't care whose idea it was," roars CardaMom.

"We've never done it before, I swear —"

"So you decide to try it for the first time when you have a guest who's never sledded before, a guest with *no helmet*?"

"What's skitching?" demands Aspen too.

Luiz's Adam's apple bulges as he swallows hard. "Super thing the friends teach me, we hold on behind the car for sled way way faster down the street, and —"

"*Super* dangerous, and completely illegal," growls CardaMom. "Catalpa, if Luiz suffers permanent eye damage, it's on you."

Sumac's mouth falls open.

"Wow," murmurs Aspen.

72

And even though she's fourteen, Catalpa bursts into tears, with big wet gasps so loud that the nurse puts his head through the curtain to see if someone's in pain.

After his bubble operation, Luiz comes out with a big patch taped over his right eye; white, so not like a pirate's, Sumac decides. His two eyes are sore and watery, because the doctor had to poke and prod them both to make sure there was no more damage.

In the taxi home, he has to sit with his face flat on his knees. (Something to do with letting liquid trickle out from behind the retina . . . which Sumac would actually rather not have known.)

"MaxiMum says your flight was canceled anyway," CardaMom tells him, glancing up from her phone in the taxi, "so you'll get rebooked once the weather improves."

Luiz manages only a small smile.

Catalpa leans her wet face on CardaMom's shoulder like she's a little girl. She's sitting on her hands so she won't rub her tear-swollen eyes, because she's afraid of dislodging her contacts.

Sumac still can't quite believe that her big sister and her friends were hitching rides behind speeding cars. That's like crossing the street on a red light, times a million!

The taxi driver keeps hissing and grunting because he says the motorway's so *treacherous*. Sumac thinks she feels the van's wheels skid on the ice, so she lets out a whimper and gets into the brace position, with her head pressed against the seat in front.

Catalpa sniffs. "That's just for airplanes, you twit."

She must be feeling a bit better if she's putting Sumac down again.

CardaMom pats Sumac's leg. "Just sit back, *kheien:a*, and your seat belt will keep you safe."

Kheien:a means daughter, Sumac remembers. She leans back and squeezes her eyes shut so she won't see other cars skating toward the taxi . . .

And the next thing Sumac knows, PopCorn's lifting her out of the cab, and icy rain startles her awake.

Luiz nearly goes splat on the front steps because his sneakers aren't grippy enough, but MaxiMum grabs him just in time.

"Geronimo!" That's Opal, overexcited, shrieking in the Hall of Mirrors. Wood probably taught him that.

CardaMom gets Luiz up the stairs and onto one of the sofas in the Loud Lounge, as he's not remotely sleepy enough to go down to the Overspill, even though it's nearly midnight. He's under orders from Doctor Yazdani to lie *prone* for the first three hours. Sumac can never remember which way up that means.

"*Prone* is facedown," CardaMom tells her, "the opposite of *supine*. Think of someone *supine* on their back — you could feed them spoonfuls of *soup*."

"They'd choke," Sumac objects.

"Fine, picture them choking — the best mnemonics are bizarre," says CardaMom.

"The important thing is for Luiz to stay leaning forward," says MaxiMum, "because gas wants to float upward, so that'll keep the bubble pressed against the top of the back of his eye."

Oh, *now* it makes sense to Sumac. Just as well he didn't tear the lower bit of his retina, she thinks, or he might have to hang upside down like a bat.

"Hey, Luiz, you're literally a couchsurfer now," says Aspen, slapping his back.

"Don't shake him," cries Sumac.

"It was just a gentle pat."

Wood and PopCorn and MaxiMum have stayed up all these hours playing Cheat and eating nachos. They didn't

75

hang around very long at the parade, because of the freezing rain.

"It starts as snow, see," says Wood, in his meteorologist tone, "then it melts as it passes through the warm middle layer of air, and then the cold air just below the ground *super*cools the droplets, so when they touch any surface, they form an icy glaze on contact."

"Like you superbore us on contact," mutters Aspen.

Sumac tries a nacho, because she knows she must be hungry, but the cheese is cold and rubbery.

"Curses!" PopCorn's staring at his phone. "Flight's canceled."

"I know it before," says Luiz, prone on the sofa cushions.

"And it's actually handy because Luiz is not allowed to go anywhere for five days anyway," says Sumac.

PopCorn's shaking his head. "PapaDum and Sic's flight from Delhi, I mean. The airport's jammed with hundreds of airplanes because it's taking so long to deice them."

"No way!" Sumac, Aspen, and Wood wail at the same time, for once in total agreement.

"Have Sic and PapaDum been rebooked on the next direct flight?" MaxiMum asks.

PopCorn nods. "They should be home the day after

tomorrow — the twenty-third." His usual smile is upside down.

Sumac's suddenly totally exhausted. She stumbles off to bed, leaving the others still chatting around their flattened guest.

In her white-and-silver bedroom at the top of the house, she lies on her back, too dizzy to even reach up and turn off her fairy lights. Then she flips herself like a pancake to try lying *prone*, like Luiz — but it presses her nose so she can't breathe, and if she turns her head it makes her neck ache. If Luiz moves his head in his sleep, will his air bubble get dislodged and bob over to the side of his eye like a bandage coming off, letting the cut in his retina sag open again? Ew!

Sumac tells herself not to worry about it: The parents will figure something out for Luiz.

But it's hard to switch off worry once it's begun. For instance, how can the Lotterys do all tomorrow's festive stuff when two of them are missing? (Like suitcases delayed in transit: She pictures her dad and big brother revolving slowly on a conveyor belt.)

She wonders if she'll be able to get to sleep at all, or if this longest night of the year is just going to go on and on and on . . .

CHAPTER 4

THE ICE STORM

I t's weirdly quiet.

When Sumac looks out her window, first thing in the morning before the sun's even up, the world's all blurry. She puts on her furry robe and her moccasins that her baba bought her when the Lotterys went to their family's reserve for the annual Powwow. She pads down one floor to the landing outside Catalpa's Turret (with its castle-style door) and the Wood Cabin (which says, in her brother's most jaggedy writing, *Keep Out: Trespassers Will Be Shot*).

From here she can see the scene in front of Camelottery, under the glow of a streetlamp. She bites her lips with excitement.

79

Every tree, every pole, every *No Parking* sign, every car, every garbage can has been thickly coated with ice. The big Manitoba maple is frilled all over. Somebody's bicycle, chained to the fence outside the rooming house next door, has been magicked into a glittering sculpture as good as any at the festival.

A funny, faint sound: *eek eek, cror cror, eek eek.* Is that the trees creaking? Sumac wonders.

Icicles dangle like stalactites from every roof on the street. The power line overhead is decorated with crystals like a string of bunting. This isn't the big snowfall Sumac was longing for, to make everything look like a Christmas card. It's stranger and even better. The city's wearing a new silver skin, and it's beautiful.

And then three things happen all in a row, right before Sumac's eyes: The Manitoba maple makes a terrible retching sound, its longest bough keels over to the side, and everything to the left of Camelottery goes dark.

Sumac gallops down through the house. She doesn't understand; how come the lights are still on here, but not in all those houses stretching down the street? What a fluke!

She crashes into Wood coming out of his room. "You won't believe what just happened."

"More than three centimeters of freezing rain in the night," he says, nodding. "The layer of ice on everything is so heavy, it's ripped down power lines across the city —"

"No, but out there, on our street," says Sumac. "I actually *saw* this huge branch fall and half the houses have gone black — our poor neighbors!"

"Yeah, and three-quarters of a million other people who don't have electricity now." Wood's hard to impress.

Sumac lets her brother do his know-it-all thing at her for a few minutes — *low-pressure systems* and *ice accretion* and *frost quakes* and blah blah blah. Then she escapes and puts her head in the moms' room.

MaxiMum is cross-legged on the neat side, facing the wall. She's recently joined a virtual sangha, a meditation group. That means she gets a text message every morning and has to go do it right away so all six group members will be meditating together even though they're in different parts of the country. "Sorry," whispers Sumac, "I do see you're busy —"

Outside on the stairs, Aspen's warbling something about *walking in a winter wonderland*.

"— only the thing is," Sumac says, "there's been a thing called an ice storm!"

"I'm aware. Is it an emergency?" MaxiMum speaks without opening her eyes or turning her head, which is a bit unnerving.

"Well, yeah, it's like a war zone out there," says Sumac. "I've been getting thrilling footage out the window. Police are putting yellow tape everywhere so nobody steps on fallen wires and gets zapped. Wood says a transformer exploded" — Sumac doesn't actually know what a transformer is, but it sounds pretty bad — "and that they're saying on Twitter that the mayor should call in the army and declare a state of —"

MaxiMum interrupts. "No, Sumac, I mean is there an immediate emergency, such as Grumps having a heart attack, and am I the only adult you can find?"

"Ah, no," admits Sumac. She waits. "So — you're saying I should go?"

More silence. Meditation means you practice choosing . . . Sumac tries to remember her mother's phrase. *Not to be disturbed by disturbances or distracted by distractions*, is that it? But the muscle around MaxiMum's jaw is making a grinding movement, as if she's feeling distracted *and* disturbed. Maybe the ice storm is stressing her out and she specially wanted to be left alone so she could calm down by meditating?

"OK, sorry, see you later," whispers Sumac, "bye!"

Down in the Mess, there are no other parents to be found. Catalpa looks up from the tablet. "They're out checking nobody's house is on fire."

"Why would ice set things on fire?" asks Sumac, bewildered.

"Hello, ripped electrical wires," Catalpa says, "sparks flying?"

"Oh."

Luiz is at the long table beside Catalpa, leaning forward with his head in his hands. Sumac wonders if he's crying . . . and then she remembers that *posture* thing he has to do for the next five days. Between Luiz's eye-mergency and the ice storm, this is quite an exciting morning.

"*Olá, amiga*," he says without looking up.

"Have you been sitting like this all night?" she asks sympathetically.

"No, I did sleep my face down in the bed for some hours, on the cushion like the mega big croissant."

That sounds like the special breastfeeding cushion CardaMom last used when Aspen was a baby — but no need to creep Luiz out by mentioning that, Sumac decides. "Can't you read with your good eye, at least?"

"Not allowed," snaps Catalpa. "The two eyes move together."

Ah, Sumac should have remembered that.

"I have to play nurse, as my punishment," says Catalpa, "so I'm trapped here, making sure the guy doesn't deviate from the correct posture."

Sumac glances at the tablet. "Ah, how come you're Instagramming photos of things covered in ice, then?"

"Well, I put my head outside for two minutes."

Brian runs in wearing pj's covered in trains, her little face stern with excitement between its two polar bear muffs. "There's a nice storm!"

"Ice," says Sumac.

"A *nice* storm, Wood says," Brian insists. "But it *not* nice, it's smashing everything to bits!"

"Has Grumps been told?" Sumac asks.

Nobody seems to know, so she goes in search of him: She loves announcing news.

In the Hall of Mirrors, Sumac almost steps on Oak. He lets out a high-pitched squeal and points at Topaz — their orange cat — who's chasing a dust bunny. (Topaz has a sister, Quartz, but she's so shy that the Lotterys hardly ever catch a glimpse of her.)

"There's our kitty-cat," Sumac tells Oak. "You saw the kitty?"

He shakes his head wisely and says, "Eh."

Sumac thinks he meant to nod, and *eh* must be *yeah*. Another word! He's already got *ba*, *nah*, *kwe*, *woof*, and *By* (for Brian). She'd like to tell Oak about the ice storm, but he wouldn't know what that is.

Her grandfather's on the treadmill on the upper landing, taking what he calls his *morning constitutional*, which means strolling at the pace of a turtle with his big padded headphones on. (Sic made him a playlist of fifteen hours of old radio comedy routines from when Grumps was young. The comedy doesn't make Grumps laugh out loud, just curl up the corners of his mouth in a wintry way.) Opal is perched on top of the little screen that shows the speed the treadmill's going.

Sumac hovers till she catches Grumps's eye . . . but then

85

she only waves. She's realized she probably shouldn't distract him with news of the crisis while he's right in the middle of exercising, because what if she makes him trip and break a hip?

Grumps waves back. "Is it now?" he asks loudly.

"What?" she asks.

"What's that?" he says, echoing her.

Sumac shakes her head.

"Speak up," says Grumps. "I didn't hear the cowbell."

She raises her voice to a shout. "It's not dinner! It's still morning and there's an ice storm."

He plucks at his earphones, pulling them halfway off his head. "What's that? Ice cream?"

"No," Sumac wails. "Never mind."

From the window, she spots Wood out in the Wild with Diamond at his heels, staring up at the heaving branches of the catalpa tree (the one Catalpa was named for) between Camelottery and the Zhaos' bungalow. It can't be safe to stand right under it. Wood's got his pants rolled up, of course; Mr. Tough Guy.

Sumac runs down through the house and out the back door onto the Derriere. Cold, damp wind slaps her in the face. "Hey," she yells at her brother, "stay away from the trees, they might fall on you!"

Wood snorts.

Sumac rushes back in to put on her coat and winter boots. She uses a key to pivot the steel studs in her soles so they stick out; she always used to fall down on icy sidewalks until she got these boots.

The wet wind makes Sumac shudder as she picks her way through the long, pale grass in the Wild; icy drips go down her neck. She flips up her hood to cover more of her, but that only shakes the water right down into the small of her back. In the distance, sirens wail. Sumac's eye is caught by red berries on a bush, each with its own lovely pearl of ice around it.

She walks over to join Wood under the big catalpa tree, squinting up at it for any sign that it's about to kill any of the Lotterys. Its ice-coated branches are groaning and lashing around. They seem saggy — have they always grown that way? Sumac should have looked at this tree more closely before the ice storm. How weird to be afraid of branches now, as if they're bombs.

"The wind's gusting up to fifty kilometers an hour," says Wood with relish. "Trees are coming down like dominoes."

Sumac shivers. The sky's a hard gray. It looks like Brian's right and somebody *broked the sun* for real.

"The storm hit hard all the way from Oklahoma to Newfoundland." Wood shows Sumac a satellite image on his phone: The ice storm is a hungry white monster.

"Kwe!" CardaMom calls a greeting from the side of the house. "Coming to help?"

Sumac and Wood hurry over.

"Only if you can both be trusted not to step on any fallen wires," says MaxiMum warningly, pointing at the ground. "Assume they're all live and can fry you."

"Is Aspen coming?" asks Sumac anxiously. She can just imagine her sister electrocuting herself for fun, like that time they were hiking and she stroked an electric cattle fence. . . .

CardaMom shakes her head. "She's agreed to stay home with PopCorn and the smalls, in exchange for half an hour of Minecraft."

The moms have two axes and a handsaw between them. They look like medieval peasants going to war.

"Why aren't we bringing the chain saw to cut up the fallen branches?" asks Wood in a frustrated tone that suggests he thought he'd get to use it.

"Can't find it," says CardaMom with a rueful grin. "PopCorn thinks he remembers bringing it to the last tool exchange, but he didn't keep a note of who he lent it to. . . ."

Wood whistles to Diamond, puts her on her leash, and they set off. The path around Camelottery looks like it's been enameled. The dog skids and slithers on her three paws.

Out in front of the house, the bit the Lotterys call the Hoopla because they play basketball there, the tarmac's one big sheet of translucent gray, littered with tree debris. The basketball hoop is webbed with silver, and so is the Lotterys' big bike cage. The *Slow Children Playing* sign — which Sumac used to think referred to Oak, or other slow kids, but it actually means you should drive slowly because kids are playing — has a delicate fringe of needles dangling from its base. The cars are all glazed too, with tiny bumps in the skin of ice coating them.

Sumac finds it helps to pretend she's walking onto a rink and take baby steps with no forward momentum. There's more freezing drizzle coming down now, so she pulls her scarf up over her nose and half shuts her eyes, squinting.

The fallen branch from the Manitoba maple is at least half a meter thick. It's lying right across the street in front of the rooming house. On the tree trunk, Sumac can see where the branch tore off: a big sore hole, the wood almost orange inside. All the hair on Diamond's back is standing up and she's barking at the fallen bough as if she's outraged that it's invaded her territory.

Harry No Name sits smoking on the stoop of the rooming house, his long braid coming out the back of his Mad Pride baseball cap. The guy's mouth moves, and Sumac has the impression he's talking to himself. She's a bit nervous of Harry No Name, but she always smiles so he won't guess. He's outside in all weathers; he and Wood should start a hardiness club, Sumac thinks.

"Harry, how's it hanging?" calls CardaMom.

"Bit of excitement this morning," he says, nodding back at her.

"Yuck." That's Brian.

"Brian!" says Sumac under her breath.

"Sorry, she just means the cigarette," MaxiMum tells Harry. "Brian's pretty hard-core against smoking."

"The kid's right," says Harry, taking one last suck before stubbing it out on the step.

The Manitoba maple's smaller branches are pressed against Mr. Rostov's house, across the street, and its twigs are tapping his dark front windows, though amazingly the glass doesn't seem to be broken. The downed power line has white cloths hanging over it — tea towels somebody's hung up? — like flags of surrender. Mr. Rostov comes out now, laden down with two big garbage bags about as big as he is.

"What's he doing?" MaxiMum wonders.

"Mr. Rostov, can we help you with your garbage?" calls CardaMom.

"Not garbage," he says scornfully in his Russian accent. "I put food from refrigerator in yard so it not spoil."

"Good thinking," says Wood.

"Not emptying freezer, not yet," Mr. Rostov adds. "Full freezer will stay cold two, three days."

"Surely the repair crews will have turned up and got your power back on by then?" says CardaMom.

"Don't count on it," says Mr. Rostov with a gloomy chuckle.

Sumac has a great idea. "Would you like some hot breakfast at our house?"

"I made porridge already on kerosene heater," he boasts. "Don't worry about me, little girl. When I was small like you I lived through the Siege of Leningrad."

Sumac doesn't know what that is, but it sounds impressively medieval.

Way down the street, she sees, a tree trunk has stoved a car's roof in. The headlights are all on — so the tree must have accidentally pressed the button for the headlights as well as crushing the car.

CardaMom and MaxiMum join some other adults who are using their tools to hack up the smaller branches littering the street, at least. Mr. Tsering — the skinny-as-a-skeleton

janitor the Lotterys know from the Community Center —
has a chain saw. (Sumac so wishes PapaDum was home
already, because he'd be so good at getting everybody working as a team.) Bigger kids like Wood drag the branches off
the street to pile in their front yards. Diamond mostly just
watches and barks, as if she's the boss.

"How can I help?" Sumac keeps asking, till MaxiMum
gives her a sack of rock salt for melting the ice off the sidewalks so they'll be less slippery. So Sumac organizes the
smaller kids to scatter the salt. She even teaches them how
it works — by lowering the freezing point of the water —
though not many of them seem to be listening.

Then the kids need something else to do. Sumac suggests they all go home to scavenge for snacks to put out for
the birds. When one boy brings licorice strings, she sends
him back for something easier to eat. The second time he
turns up with roast-lamb-flavored chips — but she guesses
the birds won't be picky.

She notices the adults getting a bit competitive about
which of their picks and scrapers, shovels and digging bars
does a better job of breaking up the ice. After a while they
need a breather, so they stand around with faces red from
cold, swapping tips for surviving in a power outage.

Sumac keeps thinking she's hearing trucks going by, or
is it the wind?

"That's generators you're hearing," says Mr. Tsering.

"Gas-powered motors," MaxiMum explains to Sumac. "They make backup electricity when there's an outage."

People have plugged them in outside their houses, Mr. Tsering says, because if you use them indoors, the fumes could poison you.

"Why don't we have a generator?" demands Wood.

CardaMom shrugs. "It's just not something we've ever got around to buying."

"Well, we should have. What if this is the start of the end of the world?"

"Son," says MaxiMum, putting her hand on his shoulder, "no need to freak out quite yet."

From the end of the lucky half of the street that still has electricity, tiny Mrs. Marikkar emerges. She's so pregnant she looks like she's got a sun-sized melon up her coat. Behind her come her five tall daughters — all wearing their funky-patterned hijabs different ways, like side-knotted or braided or turban-style, except the youngest two, who don't wear one yet. They're carrying paper plates of little cones that smell delicious.

"How're you doing?" CardaMom's asking Mrs. Marikkar.

"Fine, fine."

"Remind me when you're due?"

94

"Not till February," says Mrs. Marikkar with a little sigh-laugh, patting her bump. "May we offer you hardworking people some short eats?"

Eyeing the cones longingly, Sumac says, "They look yum . . . but our house still has power."

"That's all right," says the middle girl, "there's plenty for everybody."

"Really? Thanks!" So Sumac has a fritter — lentil, maybe? — and moves on to a bowl-shaped pancake with an egg cooked into the bottom.

Aspen's emerged from Camelottery, wearing several scarves (including two of Sumac's), and doesn't seem to have electrocuted herself so far. She's tucking in to the fried chickpeas and giggling a lot with the Marikkar twins.

"Do you mind my asking, what are you?" the eldest girl asks MaxiMum.

"What kind of what?" says Sumac.

"Like, why are we different colors?" Wood sounds bored of that old question.

"No, no," says the girl awkwardly, "I mean are you celebrating Christmas this week — are you Christians?"

"We're kind of a mix," CardaMom tells her. "I'm a lapsed Catholic Mohawk. PopCorn was raised Presbyterian but he's basically pagan now, and PapaDum's . . . I guess you'd say a nonpracticing Hindu."

"MaxiMum's a Buddhist," Sumac puts in helpfully.

"That's not really a religion," says MaxiMum.

"Isn't it?" Sumac's confused.

"We don't believe in a god or a soul," MaxiMum tells her.

"Huh. What is it, then?"

"Something you practice, I guess," says MaxiMum. "A technology."

Wood overhears that. "Like Xbox?"

"Sure," says MaxiMum. "A technology for being happy."

"So, exactly like Xbox," he says.

Mrs. Marikkar has her head on one side as if she doesn't know what to make of them. "And you boys and girls?"

"I'm an atheist," says Wood.

Really? Sumac didn't know that.

"We're mostly electric," says Aspen.

Sumac wonders if she's talking about the power outage.

CardaMom lets out a hoot. "You mean picking and choosing from different traditions?"

"Yeah, and making up our own minds," says Aspen.

"Then the word you want is *eclectic*."

"Whatever," says Aspen, mouth full again.

"Anyway," Sumac tells Mrs. Marikkar, "we'll definitely have a special Christmas dinner on the twenty-fifth, with a gigantic roast turkey and cranberry sauce and about ten different vegetables and mince pies and plum pudding and crackers." The Lotterys always set places for their dead people too: MaxiMum's dad, and PopCorn's and CardaMom's moms, and PopCorn's ex-boyfriend Michael.

"Crackers with, ah, cheese?" asks Mrs. Marikkar.

"No, the kind you pull. They go bang and bad jokes and toys fall out," Sumac tells her.

Mrs. Marikkar's looking puzzled. "The jokes must be bad?"

Sumac shrugs. "They just always are."

"Not as bad as yours!" Aspen mumbles. "Sumac's jokes are the unfunniest ever."

Luckily, Sumac tells herself, Aspen's got so much food in her mouth, the Marikkars probably don't understand a word she's mumbling.

Then Ben and Baruch from two streets over turn up, looking for Sic. They say their street has no fallen trees and is frozen into a perfect rink. Wood grabs his skates from the house and skates off to play shinny (ice hockey) with them and their friends.

Mr. Zhao emerges from his bungalow next door, with a huge pot of boiling water to pour over the wheels of the Poop Cube, which have frozen to the ground. (The Poop Cube is what the Lotterys call the nasty brown car that

Mrs. Zhao gives Sic driving lessons in.) When his wife comes out with two suitcases, he says something in Mandarin and points up at a white pine that must be twenty-five meters high. It's standing perfectly straight, but there's one big branch that's arching over their street, and waving in the wind.

The Zhaos still have power, like the Lotterys, but they're packing up to go stay with their son because in his suburb the power lines are underground, so none of them got ripped down.

A couple from the unlucky end of the street says their daughter is expecting them for Christmas, but they won't be able to get their car out past the big fallen maple, and it's probably too dangerous to drive on these icy streets anyway, and they've heard public transit is all canceled.

Mrs. Zhao won't change her mind about driving off to stay with their son. "Getting out of here before something else happen," she says ominously.

When Sumac, Aspen, CardaMom, and MaxiMum come indoors to take off their soaked things and warm up, they find PopCorn's baking some kind of muffins.

Sumac just hopes they won't be too experimental. She wipes a smear of batter off PopCorn's stubbled cheek. "We invited Mr. Rostov in, but he says he doesn't need any help because he survived something called the Siege of Leningrad," she reports.

Grumps's eyebrows go up. "Ate cats, so they did."

Sumac frowns. "You sure it's cats you're thinking of, Grumps?" Is this one of his dementia-brained moments?

"Check your history books," he insists. "Cats, dogs, rats, toothpaste, and sawdust and glue."

PopCorn gives Sumac the little nod that means *It's all true.*

Brian's on the floor, busy wrapping presents — random objects that she covers in paper and string and tape, and then she gives them to you and shouts (in a stern voice), "Present!" And you have to somehow get the thing open and seem very excited and grateful, whatever it is. (Sometimes Brian puts random letters on the paper — because she can't read yet — and demands, "What I writed?")

Luiz is still leaning forward with his head in his hands. Catalpa raps the table to get his attention. "Do you remember all our names yet? PopCorn . . ."

". . . PapaDum, CardaMom," Luiz

chants. "Hey, they are all called for the foods! Or no, not all."

Just then, MaxiMum comes through the Mess with a tray of dirty dishes she's collected from all around the house.

"The dads, they are crunchy food," Luiz tells her, "and your CardaMom, she is the spicy. So you, why aren't you to eat?"

MaxiMum grins. "The thing is, Luiz, the four of us made a deal to live together and raise some kids," she says, stacking plates in the dishwasher. "We never agreed to be the same."

"You could be . . . SalaMammy, like the salami," he suggests.

"SalaMammy!" crows Brian.

"That's superb," says Catalpa. "Or what about . . . MaTzo Ball?"

"MaRaschino Cherry?" suggests Sumac.

"That's actually quite good," says Catalpa in a surprised tone.

But MaxiMum has headed out the door already.

"SalaMammy!" Brian's still sniggering.

"OK, the kids' names now," says Catalpa, clicking her nails on the table under Luiz's elbows again. "We're all trees, or we were originally: Sic is Sycamore, Wood's actually Redwood, and Brian used to be Briar."

"Ah, by the way . . . I think Brian is boy name, no?" asks Luiz.

"Yeah," Brian pipes up from the floor. "Not a girl." She's got a long piece of tape tangled around both her fists now.

Luiz nods as if he's getting his head around that. "But, excuse me, you all say *she*?"

Sumac sees what he means. "Hey, Brian," she asks, "do you mind when we call you *she*?"

Brian frowns, either because she's thinking hard or because she's wrestling with the tape.

"Do you want us to say *he* or *they* or something else instead?" asks Catalpa.

During the Indigenous Peoples of the World festival, Sumac remembers, CardaMom brought home a theater director who went by *they* instead of *she* or *he*. At first it felt funny to say *they* about one person, but the Lotterys soon got the knack.

"Nah," says Brian now. "Get me out!"

"OK, OK," says Sumac, "let me find where it starts."

She picks at an edge of the tape, but Brian's so wriggly, finally Sumac just has to peel the whole tangle off, with Brian going "Ow ow ow" all the way.

Now Catalpa helps Luiz post a looming selfie of his taped eye on Snapchat, with an animated arrow, and a scribbled caption in Portuguese that he spells out for her.

Aspen comes in and looks over their shoulders. "Want to take an ussie with handsome Slate Frisby?" She offers the rat on the flat of her hand.

"Ah, no thank you," says Luiz, leaning away.

"Aspen!" That's PopCorn, sounding unusually cross. "Keep Slate out of people's personal spaces."

On Aspen's hand, Slate is grooming himself with small, fastidious movements.

"I'm not scared . . . but in Rio we kill the rats, not cuddle," says Luiz.

"Why?" cries Aspen, shielding Slate with her body as if their couchsurfer is an axe murderer.

"Well, in my favela — like, the slum? Many living very close? — the rats are biting the children and give them the fever, sometimes to the death."

Sumac didn't know a favela could be like that. Did he not get enough food, is that why he's so small?

Oak crawls in. He bangs his sippy cup on the floor three times, then drinks from it.

"Present for Oaky-doke," announces Brian, handing him one of her sticky-tape parcels as big as his head.

Oak rolls his cup away and takes the pretend present.

"Say thank you," she tells him.

Oak actually does say something like *agoo*, so they all clap, which makes him laugh and drop the parcel.

"Another word!" says Sumac.

"Oak will talk when he's good and ready," CardaMom reminds her with a grin.

"Yeah, but it's fun," says Sumac. "When he's grown up I'll show him the list of the first twenty things he said."

Somewhere on the side of the refrigerator is a list of her big brother Sic's first fifty. But after that the dads and moms got too busy.

Sumac reads Doctor Yazdani's printout to check Luiz is obeying all the rules. He has to sit leaning forward for at least sixteen hours out of twenty-four. He can listen to music, or watch TV on a device on the table — in fact, TV is actually recommended, like a medicine! — but no sports, no dancing. "You're not even allowed to play cards or knit, Luiz."

Wood sniggers. Sumac hadn't realized he was back from playing shinny.

"FYI, lots of very hip guys knit these days," Catalpa tells their brother.

"Only the kind you hang out with," says Wood.

"Well, if society breaks down as a result of environmental collapse," says Catalpa, "you're going to need to make your own clothes out of weeds and stuff."

Sumac and Aspen share a smirk at that image: Wood in knitted weeds!

"Doing all right?" Catalpa asks, leaning her head close to Luiz's tilted one.

He lets out a tiny groan. "I feel so disgust. I never go to the bed with no shower before this last night."

That surprises Sumac.

"Luiz was telling me that in Brazil, in the summer, people sometimes have four showers a day," says PopCorn.

Sumac studies the list. "You are allowed a bath if you don't get your broken eye wet, Luiz, but not a shower — too splashy, I guess. No electric razors — because of the vibration."

"We've got some disposables," PopCorn assures him.

"And we're to watch him for complications," Sumac adds. That must mean things that turn out to be more complicated than you expected — like Grumps's cross-words, which he always seems to leave half-done these days. The list of things that could happen to Luiz's eye is scary:

> infection
> cataracts (Aren't they waterfalls though? Sumac
>   wonders)
> glaucoma
> bleeding into the eyeball

loss of vision

loss of eye

Sumac lets out a yelp. "Luiz, it says here you could lose your —"

PopCorn bulges his own eyes at her, and Sumac takes the hint and shuts her mouth.

"Doctors have to warn you about every bad thing that could possibly happen," murmurs PopCorn, "so you won't sue them. It's like those forms we have to fill in before you guys try something fun like ziplining, saying we know you might end up dead."

"I so want some time to do the ziplining," says Luiz, as if he's an old man who'll never do anything fun again.

Oak reaches out for Sumac's knee and staggers over to her, planting his plump face in her ribs.

She kisses him on the top of his spiky hair.

"Hey, it's time for your medication again," Catalpa tells her patient.

Luiz straightens up and picks at the edge of the white tape, then lifts his patch. He leans back, blinking. The white of his eye is half-red . . .

"This won't take a second," murmurs PopCorn, unscrewing the dropper from the little bottle.

Sumac and Catalpa both look away squeamishly as the drop falls into Luiz's eye.

"I am sorry to be trouble," says Luiz.

"No trouble at all," PopCorn tells him.

"What's up with the lad?" asks Grumps, wandering into the Mess.

The Lotterys explain, yet again.

Oak pulls himself upright on Grump's trousers. Grumps bends over to flip Oak's soft ears. "Count yourself lucky," he tells Luiz.

"Why lucky, Mr. Grumps?" This is one of their names Luiz has no trouble remembering. He must think it's a surname, because he always respectfully adds *Mr.* to it.

"I had to stay prone for three weeks after an eye operation one time," says the old man. "My whole face swelled up like a hippopotamus."

"Ouch," murmurs Sumac. Funny that Grumps can remember fancy words like *prone* and *hippopotamus*, but not much easier things like the way to the convenience store. Last month he *nipped out* to buy cigarettes, and when the Lotterys tracked him down by the GPS chip in his watch, Grumps was striding along the lakefront, about ten kilometers from home.

Holding on to Grumps's index fingers, Oak bounces his knees like a tennis player staying limber.

"Excellent standing, Oaky," says Sumac.

"Eh," he says, for *yeah*.

"One of these days you'll be walking," she tells him, to help herself believe it.

At the table, Luiz lets his face drop onto his folded arms.

"Is your eye hurting?" Catalpa asks.

"No, just the other bits of me." He pats his arms, his neck, his shoulder blades, and spine. That's most of him, Sumac thinks: the poor guy!

Catalpa looks up from her screen. "Score! There's a place right here in Toronto that rents out equipment for convalescing after eye operations. They've got a special chair like massage therapists use at airports, and a facedown sleeping pad, and a reverse mirror for looking up . . ."

"Clever girl," marvels PopCorn. "Though I fear they'll be shut because of the weather."

"Oh," says Catalpa, downcast.

Sumac's reading a more cheerful Greek myth today, about a pair of oldies called Baucis and Philemon who are the only ones in town kind enough to take in two strangers for the night. But at dinner Baucis notices that even though she keeps filling up the strangers' wine goblets, the jug never gets any emptier . . . and, ta-dah, the visitors turn out to

107

be gods (Zeus and Hermes) in disguise! Only it gets gory again at the end, when the gods smite everybody else in town with a terrible flood for not having enough *xenia* — that's a special Greek word for guest-friendship or being welcoming.

As Sumac heads downstairs, she wonders if maybe Luiz was sent to test the Lotterys for *xenia*? In which case, all they've managed so far is to tear his eyeball, so they'd better look after him properly from now on. . . .

Lunch was meant to be saltfish (national dish of Jamaica), but that takes three days to soak, so MaxiMum's made rice and peas — very peppery, which makes Sumac sneeze.

Luiz comes in all shakily, leaning on the wall and on Catalpa. He claims lunch is *super tasty*, but Sumac's not convinced he really means it.

Harry No Name and Mr. Tsering both really love it, though. (A handful of the power-outage neighbors have come in for lunch.) Mr. Tsering turns out to have a wife — she's not well, so she's gone to a Warming Center today — and three jobs: school janitor, cleaner in a laundromat, and restocker in a big-box store. Sumac wonders when he sleeps.

"Where did you get your mysterious name?" Aspen's asking Harry No Name as he drains his second coffee.

He lets out a little huff of laughter. "I'm from Southern

Saskatchewan, me. The Indian Agent — the white man sent to boss us around, right? — he couldn't spell my ancestor's name, so what he wrote down was *No Name*."

"But what was it?" asks Aspen. "Your ancestor's real name."

Harry shrugs, and carries his empty plate to the sink.

"Want to stay a while, Harry, keep warm?" CardaMom asks him.

He shakes his head. "Thanks, but — things to do."

"Me too," Brian assures him. "I wrap presents."

"'Tis the season, all right," says Harry. "I'm off to the One Dollar."

That's the café around the corner where you pay what you can — only a dollar if that's all you can spare. "Didn't you get enough lunch?" asks Sumac. "There's more in the pot."

"I work there," Harry tells her.

When he's gone, CardaMom explains that Harry used to eat at the One Dollar Restaurant after he got out of the psychiatric hospital, but then the Franciscan friars who run it heard about his years of experience serving meals when he was in jail, so they got him to volunteer there.

109

"What are friars?" Aspen wants to know.

"Mobile monks — the out-and-about kind, you know?" says CardaMom.

"With a rope for a belt, like Friar Tuck in the Robin Hood stories," says Wood.

MaxiMum and PopCorn are off to the hardware store around the corner to buy more salt to scatter on the steps of Camelottery. Also those little plastic bags that have chemicals inside that warm your hands and feet when you scrunch them. "And maybe a bucket of chicken wings?" Wood calls after them.

"You just had your lunch," MaxiMum points out.

"It's an emergency situation."

She laughs hollowly.

But when she and PopCorn come back, they're empty-handed, because the power was out in the hardware store too. Desperate customers were lining up to be led through two by two by an employee with a flashlight, they report, and all payments had to be in cash.

It's like one of those depressing YA novels set in a terrible future. Sumac's suddenly noticing all the things that use electricity in Camelottery: the microwave, and the lights, and the Wi-Fi. . . . She wonders aloud, "How would people manage if there wasn't any power at all anymore?"

"Die out," says Wood with a shrug.

Sumac goggles at him. "Really?"

"How d'you think all your ancestors somehow made it through to the twentieth century without electricity?" asks CardaMom.

"Yeah, but we've forgotten how. Gone soft," says Wood. "Nature will love it when we filthy humans are all gone."

Sumac's eyes are bulging with fright.

"I bet we'd figure something out, *tsi't–ha*," says CardaMom, giving her a one-armed hug.

CHAPTER 5

- -

GOOD KINGS WENCESLAS

U p in the Loud Lounge, Sumac considers her calendar. The ice storm may be an exciting kind of drama, but it's pretty inconvenient. She heaves a sigh and draws a thick line through *The Nutcracker* because the ballet will be canceled — but then, looking on the bright side, the Lotterys didn't even have tickets anyway. Here's a bigger problem that's just occurred to Sumac: How can they go cut down a Christmas tree when they can't use a car-share to get out to the tree farm, because so many streets are closed off?

"Who hasn't done their Lots yet?" yells CardaMom, below.

Sumac caps her pen reluctantly. Chores — really, could anything be less festive?

On the stairs, Oak is standing up, nearly straight, without holding on to anything. CardaMom holds her right arm behind him in case he topples backward. With the other hand, she holds out the black satin hat with the slips of paper inside.

The Lotterys always pick their chores from an old top hat, to make it more like Hogwarts. They call them Lots because that means your fate or luck, like a *lot*tery ticket.

Catalpa is there already, patting the next step to encourage Oak to climb it.

Instead, he slaps it too, as if this is a drumming game, and giggles.

Catalpa pulls a slip of paper out of the hat and makes a face. "Poop duty, seriously? I'm full-time nursing our wretched Brazilian, anyway."

"He'd be in Paris climbing the Eiffel Tower by now if you hadn't taken him out doing illegal stuff," Sumac points out.

"Actually, I did all the pet litter boxes already," MaxiMum calls down from the moms' room.

Catalpa smirks.

"You're a star," CardaMom calls back to MaxiMum, "but you're also messing up our system."

MaxiMum appears on the landing. "Yeah, well, I thought if I had to smell that cat box one more day I'd explode."

The thought of the serene MaxiMum exploding alarms Sumac. "It wasn't me who was in charge of the litter last week," Sumac assures her.

From the stairs above, Aspen sniggers, which Sumac takes as a sign of guilt.

"There must be an app for that," says CardaMom with a grin. "Family scheduling software, but retrospective, to keep track of who's failed to do what."

"We could call it QuikFault," suggests Catalpa.

"Or iBlame," says Aspen.

"Yeah, I like iBlame," says MaxiMum.

Aspen comes down and pulls an easy Lot: *Roll everyone's sacks of laundry downstairs to Sock Heaven.* (The Lotterys call the basement room with their washer and dryer in it Sock Heaven, because they pin up any odd socks on the corkboard.)

Whereas Sumac gets *Mop the Mess*, grrr.

Still, she really has to be helpful today, so the holidays will go as smoothly as possible in spite of the ice storm, and no parents will explode.

Down in the Mess, Sumac rubs all the stickiness off the floor with the squeezy mop, pretending hard that she's

Quvenzhané Wallis in the movie *Annie*. She sings "It's the Hard-Knock Life," but only silently, because Luiz is there. His face is resting in a weird contraption propped on the long table: the "croissant" cushion, plus two regular ones, plus some of that giant bubble wrap the Lotterys' last lamp arrived in, topped with a plush, purple, horseshoe-shaped travel pillow, all roped together with the three-meter scarf that their gram knitted Catalpa for last Christmas. "That doesn't look a hundred percent comfortable," says Sumac.

"Is not bad, really," Luiz tells her.

"Lift your feet?" she asks. He does, and she slides the mop under.

"See, I am watching the soccer with my good eye," he says, showing the tablet tucked inside the cushion pile.

"Hey, when your match is over, can I see what Rio looks like?" asks Sumac.

"Yeah yeah, I pause." Luiz taps a few words into the tablet and slides it over. "Here is my favela."

Sumac's startled by how pretty it is: a ramshackle, medieval-looking city on a hill, but multicolored, made of tiny buildings jumbled and stuck together, cascading higgledy-piggledy down the hillside. Hundreds of power wires dangling like tangles of a giant's hair over passageways barely wide enough to duck through. "Wow."

The Skype icon reminds Sumac —

She puts her head out into the Hall of Mirrors and finds PopCorn scrawling his latest quote on a skinny rectangular mirror.

Rough weather
Makes sturdy timber.
(Ancient Chinese Proverb)

Sumac puzzles over it. "That's not actually true, though. Rough winds break trees, don't they?"

"Ah, but if the trees get used to those winds every day from when they're tiny wee saplings," says PopCorn, "they grow up all wiry and able to resist them."

"Is that a metaphor?" Sumac asks suspiciously. "Kids should suffer a lot so they'll be tough?"

PopCorn's face puckers. "Ah, no. The wind doesn't mean suffering, exactly, just . . . challenge."

"Anyway," says Sumac, "is it time to try PapaDum and Sic yet?"

"Good idea, morsel," says her dad, going ahead of her into the Mess. "Where's a screen?"

"Here, I have," calls Luiz.

"Sorry to interrupt your match again," says Sumac as she collects the tablet from him.

"No worries, it is old one, I know Brazil wins."

Sumac runs up and down the house summoning siblings and mothers to the Theater, where they all pack in to video-call Delhi.

It's tonight — Sunday night — there already, and PapaDum and Sic are packing their bags.

The sight of them hurts Sumac in her ribs.

"Namaste!" calls Sic on the screen, bowing with his hands together. (Their big brother collects languages; he can say *My gorilla is hiding in your wardrobe* in sixteen of them.) He and PapaDum are both wearing long collarless kurtas over their jeans like locals.

"Hey, kiddos! Hi, Oak!" PapaDum blows a kiss.

Oak hoots with merriment and tries to blow one back, clapping his hand over his mouth.

"We miss you guys so much. You're too far away!" Sumac is nearly shouting.

"And vice versa," says PapaDum.

"There's actually a wise old Hindu saying, *Dilli abhi door hai*," Sic pronounces carefully. "Which means, Delhi's still very far away — like, the job's not done yet, don't count your chickens."

"Now tell us about the ice storm," says PapaDum.

The Lotterys jostle for room in front of the webcam, so they can give the most dramatic details. Sumac starts describing how she actually saw the huge branch tear off the Manitoba maple —

"Ow," cries Brian, "you're hurting my life!" She pokes Sumac hard with her pointy elbow.

Sumac moves sideways, out of Brian's way, till only one of Sumac's ears shows in the little rectangle of what-Sic-and-PapaDum-can-see.

"The roads are impossible — multicar pileups all over the city," MaxiMum's telling them.

Brian pipes up: "We have a surfer."

"What's that, *beta*?" calls PapaDum. *Beta*'s a pet name his parents called him.

"Surfer on the *couch*," she explains.

"Yeah, but isn't Luiz gone by now?" asks Sic.

"Catalpa broked him," Brian reports, pointing one accusing finger.

"Just a slight rip in his eye," protests Catalpa.

"Whoa, sis, did you punch the guy?" Sic asks.

"Sledding accident," she says in a very small voice.

MaxiMum gives her a look.

Catalpa corrects herself. "A sledding . . . incident. Pretty much totally my bad."

"Ouch!" says PapaDum.

"To make amends, I have to be glued to his side and fetch and carry for *five days*, to make sure he heals properly," Catalpa complains.

"You volunteered," says PopCorn.

She rolls her eyes. "Right, I got volunteered."

"So we'll get to meet Luiz when we fly in tomorrow, *excelente*," says Sic. "I can try out my Portuguese."

"Your seven words of Portuguese!" says Catalpa.

Their grandfather pads by the door of the Theater.

"Want to Skype, Grumps?" Brian calls.

"Do I what, now?" The old man puts his balding head in. He's got a mug of tea that might be a cold one from yesterday, Sumac thinks, because he's always leaving them around the house. The mug is one Sic printed him for his recent birthday: It says *Ageing's Great, Considering the Alternative*.

"Talk on the phone, Dad, but using the computer," says PopCorn. "Look, it's PapaDum and Sic."

Grumps squints at the waving figures on the small screen. "Thought they were in, ah, foreign parts."

"Yeah, there they are in India right now."

He laughs under his breath, as if they're all pulling his leg, and walks off.

"Tāyalet kahān hain?" asks Sic, with an agonized expression.

"Is that more Hindi?" asks Sumac.

"Guess what this one means," says PapaDum, chuckling.

Sic crosses his legs and says it again, faster: *"Tāyalet kahān hain?"*

Tāyalet . . . That sounds like *toilet* to Sumac. "You want the washroom?"

On the screen, Sic applauds. "Very useful phrase, on-site."

"Listen to you, *on-site*," scoffs Wood. "Like you're some hardened builder, instead of a teen nerd on a volun-cation."

Unsquashed, as ever, Sic strikes a muscleman pose. "Check out these biceps. Today I got to try a pneumatic drill."

Sumac frowns. That doesn't sound one bit safe. "Do you always make him wear a hard hat on the construction site?" she asks PapaDum.

"Nah," says Sic, "it flattens my fro."

PapaDum leans in quickly. "He's kidding! Everyone wears a hard hat." Then he starts going on and on about the particularly efficient toilets they've been putting in these apartments for families who've been kicked out of the slums, funded by an IT billionaire who grew up in a slum himself, and something called a living roof, which as far as Sumac can tell is made of plants. (Is that possible? Wouldn't it be squishy?)

It occurs to Sumac to wonder if her dads and moms ever regret having given up their jobs seventeen years ago to be nonstop parents. PapaDum seems happy as a clam today, like he's enjoying being a construction boss again so much, he doesn't even care about missing half the winter holidays back at Camelottery.

And now Sic's enthusing about a eight-hour bus ride they took to Shimla, where PapaDum was born, and all their amazing uncles and aunts and cousins, and the food, blah blah blah blah blah . . .

"This ice storm is messing up our traditions," Sumac says, cutting into the middle of one of his sentences. "We may not be able to get a Christmas tree, even."

"Hey, we could dig a little fir out of the Wild," says Aspen, jerking her head toward the back of the house.

Wood clicks his tongue with irritation. "The ground's frozen, and anyway, even if we could, we'd probably kill it."

"Christians over here decorate mango or banana trees instead — often with garlands of marigolds," remarks PapaDum.

"Cool," says Aspen. "Wish we had a mango tree. Then Luiz could get his juicy fruits every day."

"Wish you here," says Brian to the screen, planting a damp kiss on it.

Sumac's in the Loud Lounge listening to the local radio news in case they say anything about Christmas trees still being on sale within walking distance of Camelottery . . . but so far it's only stuff about lots more outages due to more non-Christmas trees toppling. The premier of Ontario's calling on city residents to deliver emergency supplies to their neighbors.

Oh, the premier doesn't mean just neighbors on your street, Sumac realizes, she means in your whole neighborhood.

She rushes off to find somebody.

Wood's in his Cabin next door, hunched over a screen. She recognizes the message board's logo. "What's up in the world of batology?" she asks.

"Chiropterology," Wood corrects her. "And since you ask, white-nose syndrome is *devastating* populations across North America."

That puzzles Sumac. "Why does it matter if bats have white noses?"

"It's an itchy fungus, and it wakes them up from hibernation, so they burn up their fat reserves and starve, *or* they stumble outside to find food and freeze."

"Oh dear," says Sumac. "Is it our fault?"

"Duh," says Wood. "We brought the fungus from Europe by mistake — one of our many."

Then she remembers to tell him about what the premier said on the radio. "A rescue mission!"

That phrase makes his eyes light up. "Like society's collapsing and we're rounding up the few survivors?"

CardaMom chuckles: She's outside on the landing holding Oak's hands for walking practice. "Actually, in a crisis you check in on neighbors so that society *won't* collapse."

"What a tip-top plan, Sumac," says PopCorn, leaning in to Wood's room. "*It's a beautiful day to save lives!*"

Which she recognizes as a quote from some TV-show doctor PopCorn's had a crush on forever.

Downstairs, the Lotterys get boots and coats and scarves and gloves on. MaxiMum insists Catalpa come along too, for a bit of fresh air.

"Luiz better stick to the rules while I'm out, though," Catalpa mutters.

"Oh, he'll be happy enough watching soccer."

"Don't move a muscle, *senhor*," Catalpa tells him, "or your eyeball will heal all jaggedy."

Luiz lifts his head from the cushion pile just long enough to grin. His face is all hot and pink-looking from the blood pooling in it. "She call herself my nurse," he tells Sumac, "but really she is the prison guard."

Aspen hands out festive hats from the Costume Trunk, to get them all into the right spirit for delivering good cheer. If she's not allowed to bring Slate, she wants to carry Opal on her shoulder — "because who wouldn't be cheered up by a parrot?" — but MaxiMum nixes that, and puts him back on his perch in the window.

"Vengeance is mine!" Opal shrieks.

Brian is furious that she has to stay home with CardaMom, till CardaMom makes her a sticker that says *Official Minder for Oak, Luiz, and Grumps*, and gives her the job of putting festive hats on those three, as well as fitting one on herself, under the earmuffs.

The crushed car across the road still has its headlights on. The Lotterys drag along one of their long plastic sleds for supplies, because it goes better than a cart on the thickly iced sidewalk. At least the wind's died down, Sumac realizes, and it's stopped that horrible drizzling.

"Elves!" That's Harry No Name, hailing them from the stoop of his rooming house. "You all look like Santa's helpers."

"That's the idea. *Now Dasher, now Dancer, now Prancer and Vixen,*" PopCorn quotes theatrically. "*On Comet, on Cupid, on Donner and Blitzen —*"

Wood claps a glove tightly over their dad's mouth. "Just stop."

"Any word on when you'll be electrified again?" MaxiMum asks Harry.

"That sounds painful," says Aspen with a snigger.

"Could be weeks, they say," he tells her.

PopCorn jumps in, gesturing at Camelottery. "We've a couch, Harry, if you —"

"Nah, that's OK, I'm sleeping at the Warming Center," he tells them.

Aspen tries pirouetting on the icy sidewalk, and falls on the third spin.

"I'll send you home," MaxiMum warns her quietly. "We're too busy — the whole city's too busy — for one of your *aspendents* today."

"OK, OK, OK," Aspen grumbles.

Opposite the drugstore, Sumac sees, crews are sawing through massive branches and putting up new poles to replace snapped ones. Wires are still dangling in some spots, and the Lottery parents lead the kids around taped-off areas as if they're going through a minefield. Aspen puts her hand on the yellow warning tape —

And Sumac yanks it away. "No going past this line or you could be zapped with a million bolts."

"By who," asks Wood, "Zeus?"

"Volts!" Sumac corrects herself. "I meant electrical volts, obviously."

Aspen fakes a yawn. "I was just going to twang it. Like a guitar," she says, flicking the plastic tape with one finger.

Sumac knows her sister's trying to rile her, so she walks away.

The rescue mission starts at the steamed-up Community Center down the street, where the six Lotterys sign in as volunteers. "You're all together?" asks the stressed-looking woman behind the desk stacked with packages. "My, what a lot of you."

"Actually, this is only half of us. And it's only a lot by Canadian standards," Sumac tells her. "The average Iraqi household is eight people."

The frown lines between the woman's eyebrows deepen. "Oh, are you" — she looks from face to face — "from Iraq?"

"No, that was just a fun fact," says Sumac.

The woman lets the Lotterys pile their sled with donated flashlights, batteries, thermal blankets, self-heating meals, sandwiches, and juice packs.

"Why are we only allowed to go to these street numbers?" Wood wants to know, reading the sheet.

"Because duh, otherwise some old lady might be driven out of her mind by different concerned citizens ringing her doorbell every half an hour," says Catalpa.

"Her doorbell won't work anyway, if the power's off," Sumac points out.

The first old lady whose door the Lotterys knock on shows off her blazing wood fire. "My late husband wanted to get rid of the fireplace, but I said, Dave, you never know."

"You could toast marshmallows," said Aspen.

"I can toast anything," said the old lady, holding up a big glossy brass fork, like something a devil would carry. "How do you think folks managed before the invention of the toaster, young lady?"

Then she and MaxiMum get into a polite dispute about whether it's safe to burn rolled-up newspapers, or whether there's a serious risk that paper might float up the chimney and set fire to the roof.

The Lotterys trudge along through the stinging cold air. "Hey, we're like King what's-his-name," says Sumac.

"King Tut?" suggests Wood, flattening himself sideways like in an Egyptian painting.

"King Kong?" Aspen makes like a gorilla.

"King Henry the Eighth, because we're so padded?" asks PopCorn, patting his coat.

Honestly, sometimes Sumac's family is like a game show. She finally retrieves the name from the back of her mind. "We're Good King Wenceslases. I mean Good Kings Wenceslas."

PopCorn laughs. In the poshest English accent he can manage, he bursts into the verse about the king and the page boy wading through the snow to visit the peasant:

> *Page and monarch, forth they went,*
> *Forth they went together;*
> *Through the rude wind's wild lament*
> *And the bitter weather.*

The kids always wince when PopCorn sings in public, especially when he does something ridiculously fancy like rolling the *r* in *through*. (With CardaMom it's even worse because she sounds professional — she volun-teaches voice and various instruments — so the song travels farther.)

"Fun fact, Wenceslas wasn't a king at all." Catalpa's reading from her phone. "Tenth-century Czech duke . . . banished his mother —"

"The cheek of him!" says PopCorn.

"— after she'd had his grandmother strangled with her own veil."

Sumac shudders.

"Ah," says PopCorn. "In that case, I suppose it's fair enough that he banished her."

The mother's veil or the grandmother's? But Sumac supposes it comes to the same thing.

"Then when Wenceslas was twenty-seven, his younger brother Boleslaw the Bad stabbed him in the head," Catalpa goes on.

That puts a smile on Wood's face. "The brother's name was a bit of a giveaway, no?"

Their neighborhood always has such an interestingly odd mixture of stores, Sumac thinks: a bait shop that sells worms, a custom eco jewelry studio where people make ear-rings out of rolled-up pages from old books, a payday loans place, an office where you can order a 3-D printed statuette of a loved one, something called a luggage liquidator . . . though today it all looks as if Godzilla has recently stomped through. The ice storm's left branches splintered like toothpicks everywhere.

This big street is nicknamed the Landing Strip because lots of immigrants settle there when they first arrive in Toronto. The zone the Lotterys are meant to be covering includes a high-rise apartment block with no power — which means the elevator's not working. So PopCorn and MaxiMum (with help from Wood and Catalpa) have to carry the sled between them up fifteen flights of stairs, like paramedics lifting a stretcher.

The corridors are dark and chilly, Sumac finds, but the big flashlights do help. When the Lotterys knock at the first door, there's no answer. "Dead?" suggests Wood in a tense whisper.

"More likely, gone to stay with family or friends who still have light and heat," says MaxiMum.

No answer at the next, or the next.

When residents do open up, PopCorn does most of the chatting. The Lottery kids mostly just stand and grin. The majority of people insist they're coping fine: wrapped up well, heating meals over kerosene lanterns or even candles. One man examines all the food on the sled, but says he doesn't like chicken or tuna or cheese or vegetables or hummus. (Sumac wonders what filling he was hoping for.)

A couple of residents get the wrong impression that PopCorn and MaxiMum are here as representatives from the government — despite having four kids tagging along. So they complain about everything from noise to smells to drug dealers to cockroaches.

If the residents who answer a door don't seem to understand PopCorn's English or bad French, and — much less likely — their kids don't either, he just holds up the food with a questioning kind of smile. The halal wraps are so popular, the Lotterys run out of them by the sixth floor, but most Muslim families say they're OK with the kosher or vegetarian ones instead.

In the passage of one small apartment Sumac counts thirteen heads — that's one more than the Lotterys, even. She never knew people were living so pressed together, just around the corner from her.

There's a surprising amount of smiling. People seem exhilarated to be coping so well with the crisis: They say "We'll live," or "Man makes plans and God laughs." But MaxiMum and PopCorn make sure everyone takes a flyer with the helpline number and the little map showing the way to the nearest Warming Center.

"Because it's only the first day," Aspen mutters sinisterly in Sumac's ear. "What if they don't get their power back for weeks?"

"I'd fill a bath if I were you, and have a bucket ready for flushing," MaxiMum tells one resident, "because your water pressure's going to drop as the reserve on the roof gets used up."

The volunteer sheet says to specially watch out for anyone *infirm*, which means too wobbly to manage the stairs, or maybe (like Grumps) wobbly in their minds. MaxiMum makes one ninety-year-old Roma man promise to call his daughter to come and get him, though he keeps insisting he's *perfectly all right*. They knock on the door of one tiny, almost bald woman who shivers a lot, and PopCorn works on persuading her to go to a Warming Center. But the woman won't budge, so all the Lotterys can do is leave her with some self-heating meals, bottles of water, hygiene packs, and a shiny thermal blanket.

"Oldies are stubborn," Sumac whispers to PopCorn.

"See," he says under his breath, "it's not just my dad."

On the cold walk back to Camelottery, Sumac feels a glow from having saved people from . . . well, having no lunch, at least. It was kind of a pity the Lotterys didn't find anyone about to die, though she doesn't say that out loud. "I like the bit in the song when the shivering

133

page steps in Wenceslas's footprints in the snow and finds them all magically toasty warm," she says to MaxiMum.

"Scientifically implausible."

PopCorn rolls his eyes at MaxiMum. "That's why it's called a miracle, you spoilsport."

"I get why the king and the page would bring the peasant meat and wine," says Wood, "but *pine logs*, really? I mean, they'd just spotted him *gathering winter fuel* in the forest he lives in . . . so it sounds like they're toting sand to a desert, no?"

"Maybe it was just some twigs and cones as a decorative filler for the hamper," suggests PopCorn.

That's true: In Sumac's experience even the most exciting gift basket has a lot of padding inside.

Wood snorts. "Yeah, well maybe Good King W. could have checked what his subjects really needed or wanted, and substituted a few high-value items for the pine logs."

"Gold coins," suggests Aspen. "Or vials of dragon's blood."

On the way home, the Lotterys pass a parking lot that usually has some last-minute scrawny Christmas trees, but there's a handwritten sign on the ice-painted fence that says *Closed Due to Weather.*

Aspen unzips her puffy coat and gives Sumac a glimpse of a self-heating meal.

"You *stole* from the hungry?" asks Sumac.

"I was curious." Which is always Aspen's defense, whatever the charge.

"Go give that back right now!"

"Hey, originally I swiped one for each of us, but I put back nine of them already," Aspen says self-righteously.

Then they turn the corner to Camelottery. Catalpa hurries into the Mess to check her patient's been *compliant*, and Aspen and Wood stay outside to do some sidewalk sledding. But Sumac's desperate for some reading time, so she goes straight up to the Bookery at the top of the house.

She loves the way the Bookery ceiling's painted like the edges of books so you feel you're hidden inside a shelf of them. (Sometimes, when she can't sleep, she imagines being four inches high, like the Borrowers.) What she's in search of now are books to make her feel Christmassy, or at least to go with the weather: *Stick Man*, *The Lion, the Witch and the Wardrobe*, the bit in *Anne of Green Gables* when Anne finally gets a dress with puffed sleeves . . . then Sumac adds *My Basmati Bat Mitzvah*, just to mix it up a bit.

Later Sumac wanders into the Loud Lounge, getting hungry. "So what are we going to have for our Saturnalia Banquet?" she asks MaxiMum.

MaxiMum is reading *Scientific American* and doesn't look up. "Eh . . . macaroni and cheese?"

Sumac scowls. "That doesn't sound very ancient Roman. Did they even have pasta?"

"I don't know, and I really don't care."

Aspen zooms through on her Rollerblades, pointing at MaxiMum. "Where's your curiosity?"

"I've temporarily mislaid it," admits MaxiMum. "I only signed up for raising the seven of you because PapaDum promised he'd be doing all the cooking. Tell you what, Sumac, why don't you go look up what ancient Romans might have eaten at a Saturnalia Banquet, and see if we have anything like that?"

Sumac does her best. She spends twenty minutes researching, then climbs on the kitchen steps to look through the cupboards. She doesn't find stewed eels or stuffed dormice (just as well!), but she does dig out lots of foods the Romans ate, such as sliced chicken and ham, bread, honey, goat cheese, eggs (she boils a dozen), sardines, honey, and lots of fruit. (No pasta, because the only kind the Romans had was fried sheets of dough.) Also watered wine for the adults.

"Salvete, omnes!" Which basically means *hi, guys*. That's PopCorn, presenting himself at the door of the Loud Lounge in his sheet-toga, with Opal on his shoulder, and one hand up in a gesture of welcome. The Loud Lounge is the only room with enough couches (once they've added some loungers and yoga mats) for all the Lotterys to recline while they eat.

"Io Saturnalia!" Sumac lets rip with the traditional call, at the top of the stairs, to summon the latecomers.

Her toga's the neatest, because she's practiced a lot. Oak is so small, he only needs a pillowcase, draped over one shoulder and safety-pinned under the other armpit. Sumac helps Luiz wind a sheet around himself, over his clothes, and actually with his curly hair he looks more like an ancient Roman than any of the Lotterys. Catalpa finally comes down looking really chic in some kind of toga-cloak-bare-arms-and-headdress outfit that uses — Sumac counts them — four sheets.

MaxiMum and Wood don't want costumes, of course, so Sumac compromises by suggesting they wear their shirts backward, because the Saturnalia festival is all about reversing things.

Wood complains his shirt is really uncomfortable that way, so he turns it around again. "The one day of the year when the Roman slaves get to whoop it up and be waited on hand and foot by their masters, and you want me to feel choked by my own collar?"

Luiz lies on his belly on the biggest beanbag, resting his forehead on his folded arms. Catalpa parks herself right beside him so she can serve him his food.

Oak thinks all the reclining is hilarious and cruises around, grabbing one Lottery's knee and then another's face to keep himself on his feet. "Ba, ba, ba."

"Want a banana?" Brian asks him, holding one up.

"Ba!"

She peels it from the bottom for him, monkey-style, because that's way easier.

"I'll do grace, shall I?" says PopCorn. He raises his glass. *"Eat thy bread with joy, and drink thy wine with a merry heart."*

"More pagany stuff, is it?" asks Grumps, leaning up on one elbow.

"That's from the Bible, actually, Dad. But it's roughly the right era for ancient Rome, at least."

"Ancient what now?"

"Saturnalia's the Roman feast of . . . doing what you like," Sumac reminds Grumps.

Oak paints his own neck with smushed banana. Their baby doesn't need a special day to encourage him to do what he likes.

The Lotterys are having dessert first, because everything has to be backward on Saturnalia. Sumac takes a big spoonful of rhubarb crisp, which is delicious but scalds the roof of her mouth. She lunges for the water jug. When she can speak again, she tells Grumps, "At the banquets they used to binge and gamble and throw nuts. . . . Oh, I forgot to bring any nuts."

"No throwing them," CardaMom warns her, "because Oak might eat them whole and choke."

"The poet, ah, Homer," says Sumac — or she's pretty sure she read it was someone beginning with an *H*, anyway — "said Saturnalia was the time of freedom. He called it December Liberty."

"Homer's Greek, not Roman, you pompoid." That's Catalpa.

Sumac can feel herself blushing.

"Let's mind our manners," says CardaMom.

"Don't have to, do I? Not tonight," says Catalpa, triumphant. "December Liberty!"

The rhubarb crisp was delicious, but eating chicken and cheese now is harder, Sumac finds. She tells herself the slice of ham is freshly sacrificed wild boar. Well, at least this is more authentically ancient Roman than macaroni and cheese . . .

She opens her eyes again and points at MaxiMum. "MaCaroni — that's another name we could have called you."

"Enough already. I refuse to be a food."

"MaxiMum, that sound more superhero," says Luiz.

"Exactly," says MaxiMum, giving him a gracious Roman matron nod.

Sumac starts telling Luiz about their Good-King-Wenceslasing this afternoon, but he's already heard it from Catalpa. He mimes knocking on a door. "In my favela, I do this for the health."

Sumac's puzzled. "You go door-to-door . . . for exercise?"

"No no, is my job. To give the peoples their medicines for the TB or HIV, you know? I say, *Bom dia, take your pill, don't forget, are you okay?*"

"Oh, cool." That sounds quite a bit more important than handing out sandwiches.

"I'd love to go to Brazil," says Catalpa disconsolately.

"Come, come," says Luiz, "I show you everything!"

Oak's mini-toga has slipped off already, leaving him in his diaper. Sumac just loves the two little dimples on the small of her brother's back, and his plumpy feet.

As for Grumps, he seems under the impression that his toga is an enormous napkin, because he's pulled it down from his shoulder and spread it across his lap. Tufts of gray hair stick out of the neck of his undershirt.

"Hey, I've got a Roman number puzzle for you all," says CardaMom.

Sumac's ears prick up. Only Sic can beat her at math, and he's not here.

CardaMom picks up a clean knife and draws *IX* in the bowl of ketchup — which means nine in Roman numerals. "How do you make that into 6 by adding just one line?"

Sumac squints at it. IXI . . . IIX . . . +X . . . VX . . . None of those are real numbers. LX is 60, not 6, in Arabic numerals. "It's impossible."

"Does the line have to be straight?" Aspen wants to know.

CardaMom grins. "Now that's what I call lateral thinking."

Sumac's mind races. DIX? That means 509. OIX? IXO? They're nonsense numbers.

"SIX!" Aspen sings, drawing a big *S* in the ketchup with her knife.

"Gross," says Catalpa, "that's been in your mouth!"

Sumac is busy trying not to resent the fact that Aspen's mind is bendier than hers, while she rewinds her embarrassingly falling-off toga.

CHAPTER 6

THE PLUNGE

Next morning, December twenty-third, Sumac wakes up and decides to be in a good mood because it's Brian and Oak's Welcome Day, and later on PapaDum and Sic will be home at last and the real holidays can begin.

Out the window, the sky is dark gray, and the street still looks like a supervillain's been through recently, smashing everything up. "Can you believe the mayor won't declare a state of emergency," Wood mutters as he passes Sumac on the stairs, "even though hundreds of thousands of people are sitting around shivering in the dark?"

CardaMom says she's on pancake duty — "Luckily that's one of the things I do still remember how to cook" — and can Sumac please go find Luiz and explain what they're celebrating?

Sumac hears laughter in the Theater. Oddly shy, she taps at the door with its glued-on red velvet curtains. She hears, "No no, *that* is the most worst ever!"

When she looks in, Catalpa and Luiz are huddled over a tablet watching a music video.

"Hey, *amiga*!" calls Luiz.

Catalpa pauses the video and looks over her shoulder. "What do you want?"

That's a snotty question, as if Sumac has to ask permission before coming into the room. It's not as if Luiz is Catalpa's couchsurfer — he's all of theirs. "How did you sleep last night?" Sumac asks Luiz.

"Much more better," Luiz says, with a thumbs-up. "Your sister, she make me a ramp for my chest with my face in the hole."

"That sounds painful," says Sumac.

"It uses the face cradle from our massage table, and PopCorn says it's *ingenious*, so there," snaps Catalpa.

"Anyway, I just came to say it's a special breakfast today," Sumac tells Luiz, "because it's two years since Brian and Oak came."

"Came to where?"

"This house, Camelottery," says Sumac.

"Ah, *compreendo*, they adopt your family? Like you, they are babies of the accountants?" Luiz sounds hopeful that he's understood, this time.

Sumac shakes her head.

"He can't see your face when you're standing behind him," Catalpa reminds her, "so you have to talk."

"Right, sorry," says Sumac.

"Oak and Brian are from a different mom," Catalpa tells Luiz.

"I get it now." He clicks his fingers. "You are all seven adopting."

"Nope," says Sumac, "just the last three of us."

"MaxiMum gave birth to the two eldest boys, and CardaMom to me and Aspen," Catalpa tells him.

"Anyway," says Sumac, "it's pancakes, so come on down."

In the Mess, the tablet pings as a message from Sic comes through, thanking them for the Saturnalia pics. "Happy Welcome Day B & O, blowing LOTS of kisses XXXXXXXX," Sumac reads aloud: "Also re: Christmas tree, remember the most important Lottery tradition — think outside the box!"

"Sic's right — we should improvise something," says PopCorn.

"Grub's up!" CardaMom, red in the face, turns off the gas flames and carries the heaped dishes over to the long table.

145

Everyone puts together their own skyscraper of little pancakes: Some are made with blueberries and strawberries and raspberries out of the freezer, some are lemon poppy-seed flavor, some banana walnut, some apple cinnamon, some with chocolate chips . . .

"Which pancakes, Grumps?" asks Sumac.

"Don't mind if I do."

"But what flavors?"

Their grandfather shrugs. "Pick me any with crispy edges, hen. By the time you're seventy-nine it all tastes much of a muchness, but I like them crispy."

Grumps is actually eighty-three, but no need to point that out. Sumac gives him a lemon pancake and a strawberry, because surely even old taste buds could recognize those?

Brian erects her and Oak's small pancake stacks with great care. "I *crave* you syrup," she says to Sumac.

Funny, the fancy words a four-year-old can pick up. Sumac passes the glass bottle over and opens the lid for her.

"No helping!"

"Sorry," says Sumac, and hinges it shut again.

Luiz is blissing out over the blueberry pancakes.

"Iawe kon," Sumac tells CardaMom. "Am I pronouncing it right?" CardaMom's been trying to teach them all more Mohawk words recently.

"*Iawe kon,* tastes good," says CardaMom, grinning back at her.

"Can I get down?" Aspen asks, her voice muffled. "Not hungry anymore." She's left one enormous bite-hole in her stack.

"Wait one second, speedy-pants. We haven't even lit the candles," PopCorn tells her.

Aspen slumps against the wall, and chews.

Brian stabs the little candle into the soaked top of her own stack, and then helps Oak do his (though between them they turn it into more of a Leaning Tower of Pisa). He gets raspberry syrup all down his arm, then licks it.

"No eating yet, Oaky!" Brian scolds her brother. "Got to light the candles for Melinda."

"Which one's Melinda?" asks Grumps, looking around.

"Brian and Oak's first mom," Sumac tells him.

Brian lights the two candles — well, really Pop-

Corn does, but Brian clutches the end of the long match and steers it. She shouts out, "Hi, Melinda!" Then she snuffs her own candle with a loud blast of breath.

Oak goes to do his, but has to be yanked away at the last minute because he's trying to kiss the flame, so he cries a bit.

Then he and Brian do the blowing together, and the Lotterys all clap, and sing "For They Are Jolly Good Fellows."

Luiz doesn't know the words but he hums along.

And Opal shrieks, "YOLO! YOLO!"

It feels so wrong to Sumac that PapaDum and Sic aren't here for Welcome Day . . . but they'll be home this evening, she reminds herself. No being glum!

Afterward, when they've all washed their sticky hands, Sumac helps Brian and MaxiMum put together the latest package of photos and cards and crafts for Melinda. The padded envelope's not very full until they add a necklace made of painted rigatoni.

Then PopCorn leans back, sits both the smalls on his belly, and begins the Welcome Day story. "On this very day, the twenty-third of December, two years ago, Keisha, your caseworker, drove you two across the city —"

"In her minivan," supplies Brian.

"That's right."

Brian doesn't actually remember because she was only two and a half; she's just memorized the story. "And my name Bree that time and Oak name is Owen."

"But you couldn't pronounce it, so you called him Owey."

"We said bye-bye, Melinda."

This is a new detail. Actually Keisha, their caseworker, was bringing Brian and Oak from their foster parents' apartment that day, but maybe that makes the story too complicated?

"That's right," PopCorn murmurs, "because she couldn't keep you safe. Melinda was sad."

Brian doesn't say anything.

Sumac pictures Melinda opening her envelope next week when it arrives in the mail. (Well, she pictures a woman: None of the Lotterys know what she looks like.) Melinda thinking about the two kids she lost, and only having cards and pictures and a rigatoni necklace. It makes Sumac feel so sorry for her, she's dizzy.

PopCorn goes on with the story. "So we all ran out of Camelottery shouting, *It's them! Hi, Bree! Hi, Owen!*"

Brian bursts out laughing. "You don't know I'm actually Brian and Oaky's Oak."

"Not yet we didn't. But we knew we were going to be your family."

And keep you safe always, with nobody shaking your brains, Sumac adds fiercely in her head.

"What I say?" asks Brian.

"Not a word, at first," says PopCorn. "You'd only met us a couple of times, so you really didn't know us yet." He mimics younger-Brian's suspicious scowl. "And then you said —"

"Owey mine!" That makes Brian laugh till she coughs.

"Yep, because he was *your* baby brother and you weren't at all sure about sharing him with us."

She scratches under one polar bear earmuff.

"Are you too hot in those, maybe?" asks CardaMom.

"Nah. What do Oak say?"

"I seem to remember he just went *gah gah gah*," says PopCorn. "But then you said something else, you said —"

"Poopy!" roars Brian.

"Because Oak had done a poop and you knew before any of us," says Sumac. Had Brian smelled it? she wondered, or heard it? Or did she just know her baby brother that well? Like telepathy, but just for poops: telepoopy.

Sumac enjoys Welcome Day so much, she'd almost like one of her own. But because she came to Camelottery on the same day as she was born, the Lotterys celebrate Sumac on her birthday, with a ritual that nobody else gets.

What happened was, it was Sic's seventh birthday a couple of days before, and he was meant to have a Zombie Party on Saturday, but it had to be canceled at the last minute when the call came from Jensen to say Nenita was in the middle of giving birth. So the Lotterys — just eight of them in those days, four parents and four sibs — had to dash to the hospital in two taxis to meet Sumac. (Sic doesn't bear a grudge against his sister — in fact, he claims she was the best present ever, even better than the Xbox.)

So anyway, when they all crammed into the little hospital room, Nenita asked the Lotterys if they'd promise to love this baby forever. And — nobody knows whose idea it was, they hadn't planned it — the eight of them put their sixteen hands together to make a sort of nest (including Aspen, though she was too small to understand what was going on), and Jensen and Nenita kissed Sumac and put her into the nest of hands.

So that's what the Lotterys do every year on Sumac's birthday, the seventeenth of May: They all put their hands together and grip tight, and Sumac takes a running jump and launches herself into the middle. It's hilarious, even though last year she did get painfully bonked in the face.

Later in the morning, Sumac stands reading the Where Board in the Hall of Mirrors. PopCorn's scribbled what looks like Tahini Lwz 2 Hospill 4 Gnck-Up. Sumac finally decodes it: *Taking Luiz to hospital for checkup.*

Then the front door opens a crack and Aspen's shrieks resound through the house: "Got a Christmas tree!"

Sumac pulls the door wide — and stares. What is *that*?

Pale gray bark with scaly ridges. Three skinny arms, all ugly angles. A few sodden leaves, yellow jaggedy ovals blackening at their edges. Like some gigantic skeleton, the thing scrapes the walls of the hall with its twigs as Wood and Aspen struggle to haul it up the stairs. "A broken branch off the Manitoba maple?" asks Sumac. "Seriously?"

"It's going to be unconventionally gorgeous," says CardaMom, grinning at the dripping branch. "Where are we taking it?"

"The Loud Lounge?" says Wood.

That's two floors up. CardaMom's mouth twists. "I'm just afraid it might smash pictures on the stairs . . ."

"Yeah, it didn't look quite so massive outside," Aspen admits.

"Then let's put it right here in the Hall of Mirrors, maybe? We could wedge it into that," says Wood, pointing to the cast-iron umbrella stand.

"Genius! Sumac," says CardaMom, "want to start fetching down the ornaments from the Artic?"

"They're stored downstairs in Gameville now," Sumac reminds her, "because we decided that all seasonal stuff counts as games."

"I knew you'd know, *kheien:a*," says CardaMom, rubbing Sumac's back before giving it a little push.

Soon Sumac's brought up six boxes of decorations — with Brian demanding to help, so Sumac gives her the less breakable stuff to carry, like lights and tinsel.

And it is actually quite fun trimming the so-called tree, which may be ugly, but at least it's really tall. (Sumac wonders why it's called trimming a tree, when that sounds as if you're cutting bits off, like a haircut, instead of hanging things on it.) She puts up all her favorite ornaments: the yeti, the shoe, the wind-up carousel, the snow globe, the gingerbread house, the long chain of reindeer in harness, the ballerina, the handprint-in-salt-dough made by each of the Lottery kids when they were small, the Ukranian web with its spider in the middle, the robin with real feathers and wire feet that cling to the stem . . .

The one Christmas decoration that has to be made fresh every year is the cranberry-and-popcorn chains, so she starts an assembly line in the Mess.

When Sumac slides the needle into a fresh, shiny cranberry, it makes a tiny juicy sound.

"You like cranberries, Slate?" Aspen feeds a big one to her rat, who's nesting in the folds of her hoodie's hood.

The needle sounds dry and squeaky going into the

popcorn. Still hot from the microwave, the popcorn's tasty: Brian eats about every second piece, and Sumac about every sixth. "I'm stabbing you, by the way, Mr. PopCorn," she tells their dad.

"Argh!" PopCorn cries, his hand on his heart, wincing as the needle goes in. "Urgh!"

Sumac has to pull the sticky thread through the popcorn pieces carefully so it doesn't crack them apart.

Aspen offers Slate one.

"Just the broken bits," Sumac tells her.

"Use the broken bits yourself! Nothing but the best for my rat." Aspen lifts Slate down to scratch his soft belly and give him a little kiss.

When the white-and-red chains are done, they hang them on the tree. Opal climbs onto a low branch and starts eating a piece of popcorn.

Now the big star.

"I do it," insists Brian.

Not even MaxiMum's tall enough to lift Brian up to the top of the tree to put the star on, so they have to fetch the stepladder from the Saw Pit in the basement.

"No helping!"

"Brian," says MaxiMum, "be realistic. How are you going to get up there without a little bit of help?"

Brian scowls, clutching the star.

"Hey, think of me as your personal elevator," says MaxiMum, making herself rectangular. She hums the kind of boring tune you always hear in elevators.

Brian sniggers at that. She steps into MaxiMum the Elevator and lets herself be lifted up the stepladder, one floor at a time, to put the star on the very top of the branch.

When it's all done, Sumac turns off the light in the hall, and their bizarre tree glitters with hundreds of tiny red and yellow and blue and green lights.

Just then PopCorn and Luiz come home and marvel at the Christmas tree. *"Wunderbar,"* cries PopCorn.

Sumac asks, "Why are you speaking German?"

"It used to be only your German ancestors who brought trees inside at midwinter," he explains. "Everyone else thought it was freaky till around 1840, when it went viral."

Luiz has the bandage off his right eye, and he's walking around the tree looking down into something shiny. "I see it upways in the down one!" Here's his proper honking laugh again, the one that used to get on Sumac's nerves, but now she's relieved to hear it again.

"What's that thing?" she asks.

"Just a reverse mirror I made him," says Catalpa smugly.

"Exceptional problem solving," murmurs MaxiMum.

Sumac examines it: a mirror tile cut into two rectangles, and duct-taped together in the shape of an open book that

Luiz holds tilted away from him, with two triangles of thick polystyrene keeping the mirrors apart. "That's very smart." Luiz can see what's in front of him by looking into the lower mirror, and the Lotterys can see his face in the upper mirror while they're talking to him. Sumac's really surprised that Catalpa managed to get the angles right — and a bit jealous.

Brian's made PopCorn sit down on the bottom step while she wraps tinsel around his head like a turban: "Human present!"

Aspen's trying to pose Slate on a high stem of the Christmas tree, but he keeps hiding behind decorations.

"Careful not to drop him," warns MaxiMum.

"Rats have survived falls from five stories up," says Aspen.

"So have some humans, but I'm not allowed to defenestrate you," grumbles Wood.

Defenestrate means pushing someone out a window, and it's probably Wood's favorite word.

"Death threats aren't allowed!" cries Aspen, pointing at him.

"So what did the doctor say about your eye?" Sumac asks Luiz.

"That we must be doing a good job of looking after him," says PopCorn, "because in her experience" — he puts on a strict voice — "young men are *rarely compliant*."

"Splendid work sitting on your butt for two days, young man," says Aspen jokingly, slapping Luiz on the back.

"Don't jolt my patient!" That's Catalpa.

"The hospital was full of twits who've nearly gassed themselves to death by using barbecues to heat their apartments," PopCorn adds.

"Full?" asks MaxiMum skeptically. "How many did you see, really?"

"Well, two at least."

PopCorn's such an exaggerator, Sumac always divides what he says by a factor of about ten.

"Also the baby," Luiz reminds PopCorn.

"Yes! We saw the most gorgeous tiny boy who got born last night by flashlight when the backup generator failed."

Luiz tries his mirror again. "This clever machine! I love," he says, giving Catalpa a kiss on the cheek.

Catalpa goes red.

MaxiMum's phone beeps with the message from her sangha group, so she goes off to sit, which is what Buddhists say for meditating.

"Hey, you'll like our Christmas pudding," Sumac tells Luiz, "because it's made of all sorts of fruits. You know, dried, then rehydrated — wetted again." Which sounds a bit of a strange thing to do to fruit, now that she's describing it, but she supposes it was a good way to preserve things, back in the day.

PopCorn's staring into space. "We did make a plum pudding this year, didn't we, Sumac?"

She frowns at him, suddenly not sure.

"Back in October," he adds, "so it would have lots of time to ripen and get tastier?"

"I don't remember helping," Sumac admits. "Maybe you cooked it when I was on a history tour with CardaMom?" Her mother does the storytelling for three-hour bus tours about indigenous life in Toronto, and she brings along Sumac to pass around the objects for handling. "Or while I was at a Saturday coding class?" Which is thirteen Pokémon-obsessed boys and Sumac in a basement, but still fun.

PopCorn chews his lip. "October was crazy busy, I seem to recall. We'd just installed my antigravity yoga sling in the Gym-Jo . . ."

Yeah, he did spend most of that month dangling upside down like a happy bat. "You mean we totally forgot to make our Christmas pudding?" asks Sumac.

His face screws up like a paper bag. "It's a food thing, and PapaDum's in charge of all that . . . but it's a British thing, so it probably should have been me."

Sumac chews her lip.

PopCorn jumps up. "I'll nip out and buy one now."

"Where?" asks CardaMom. "Pretty much everything's shut."

"Anyway, that's cheating," Sumac points out, "because we're meant to stir all the good luck of the year into it."

"OK, forget it. My bad." Sounding quite unlike himself, PopCorn flops into the chair.

Catalpa speaks without looking up from her phone. *"Last-Minute Christmas Pudding."*

"No such thing," says PopCorn tragically. "It takes a day to soak the ingredients, another day to steam . . ."

"One hour total prep, guaranteed delicious," Catalpa reads aloud.

Sumac leans over her sister's shoulder to see the list of ingredients.

Luckily, PapaDum always keeps the cupboards of the Mess well stocked. One time he was able to feed the family plus Sic's entire SSSC (Safe Streets for Skaters and Cyclists) group at half an hour's notice.

PopCorn pulls out the biggest mixing bowl they have — Oak sits in it sometimes to play — and the Lotterys chuck in all the dried fruit they have. It's a pretty odd combination: apricots, sultanas, sour cherries, raisins, dates, cranberries, and orange peel, with jars of mincemeat. "Why are there no actual plums in plum pudding?" Sumac wants to know.

160

"It's ye olde word for raisins," PopCorn tells her. "Now, rustle me up anything we have in the nut line."

Sumac finds rather elderly pecans, salted cashews she rinses the salt off . . . and she decides to count pine nuts, which are technically seeds.

Butter, sugar, flour, eggs, lemon juice . . .

Catalpa whizzes some ends of loaves from the freezer into breadcrumbs, though the food processor shakes wildly, as if it's chewing through concrete.

Nutmeg, cinnamon, baking soda, vanilla . . .

"Won't a whole cup of brandy make the pudding taste alcoholish and yucky?" asks Sumac, putting up her hand to stop PopCorn.

"No no, it harmonizes the flavors," he assures her, sloshing the brandy in.

They each take a turn stirring the pudding clockwise because that's the tradition. You really have to push; Sumac can feel it in her belly muscles. She thinks of Sic on the outskirts of Delhi mixing up cement that will hold people's apartments together for the rest of their lives. It occurs to her that the plane must be cutting through the cold sky over Greenland right about now. *Come home soon and safe* . . .

Brian stirs so enthusiastically that pudding mix nearly climbs over the rim of the bowl.

"Wait! The lucky things!" Imagine if they'd forgotten

to put them in. Sumac licks goo off the heel of her hand and runs to search for the thimble, ring, and coin. She finds them in a little bag at the back of the baking things drawer, after nearly slicing her wrist open on a maple leaf cookie cutter.

"Me throw them in!" Brian yells.

"Not so much throw as gently *drop* them in, OK?" says PopCorn.

Brian chucks the lucky things hard, like pebbles, but they do all land in the bowl. Then she — two hands on the wooden spoon, and her face puckered as if she's bench-pressing a hundred kilos — pokes them into the mix. (With PopCorn adding a few more strokes with the spoon, once Brian's not looking, to make sure one Lottery won't end up with all the luck.)

Sumac's already brushed the cooking bowl with melted fat, so PopCorn can pour the pudding in — or rather, he holds up the huge mixing bowl and tilts it, while the kids attack the goo with various implements to persuade it all to drop out.

"Now all it needs is twenty-five minutes in the micro-wave," says Catalpa, as Diamond helpfully licks a glop of pudding mix off the floor.

PopCorn suddenly clicks his fingers. "Munchkins, I've an idea for a brand-new holiday tradition. What if we —"

Aspen interrupts. "All played Minecraft at the same time!"

"No no, listen," says PopCorn, "why don't we read *A Christmas Carol* aloud?"

A chorus of groans. Their dad proposes this every year. Sumac hasn't actually read the book, so all she knows is that it's by Charles Dickens ("greatest novelist *ever*," as PopCorn always adds). And that there's a crotchety old miser called Ebenezer Scrooge and some ghosts who scare him into being more festive.

PopCorn pushes his lower lip out and makes it quiver. "The only reason I had kids was so that someday we could act out *A Christmas Carol* together." He kisses the sticky tufts of Oak's hair and fakes a sob. "That's been the vision that's kept me going, all these grueling years . . ."

"Never going to happen," Wood tells him, "so stop humiliating yourself by asking."

"Hard-hearted Grinches, the lot of you!"

That one Sumac *has* read: *How the Grinch Stole Christmas*. She loves the bit when the Whos wake up to no presents, and manage to sing anyway.

"My dream of parenthood was more like *The Sound of Music*, because that was the first film I ever saw in a movie theater," says CardaMom reminiscently. "I thought it'd be all about cycling through the countryside, yodeling, putting on puppet shows . . ."

On Christmas Night, that's what the Lotterys always do. Not cycle through the countryside, but stream *The Sound of Music* and sing along at the top of their voices. Sumac's favorite character is Brigitta, because they're both the fifth of seven, and excellent noticers.

"What else is exciting of today?" Brian wants to know.

"Eh . . . that's about it, now," Sumac tells her. "We had your Welcome Day breakfast, *and* put up the tree, *and* made the pudding."

"But what in the calendar," says Brian, knocking discontentedly on the cardboard like it's a locked door.

Sumac points to Polar Bear Plunge. "Well, I was planning to go video PopCorn and Wood jumping into the lake to save the polar bears — but that'll be canceled because of the weather." She feels in her pocket for a pen to draw a line through the words.

"Are we a hundred percent sure about that?" asks Wood.

Brian's frowning. "Bears be drowning?"

"What?" says Sumac.

"Don't they know swimming like me?"

"Actually, they swim much better than we do," says MaxiMum. "The humans don't save the lives of the polar bears, they just raise money to protect their habitat and help them not go extinct."

"Oh," says Brian, in a tone that could be relieved or disappointed.

Wood glances up from his phone. "Actually, the Plunge is still on."

"Huh." MaxiMum shakes her head in disbelief.

"Well, I suppose anybody tough enough to jump into one of the Great Lakes in late December can't be put off by a few little inconveniences like blackouts and a transit shutdown," says CardaMom.

"PopCorn? It'd only take us about half an hour to walk to the beach," says Wood.

"Do it," cries Sumac. "They *are* going to jump in the lake!" she tells Brian.

"Swimming with the polar bears!" Brian tickles her earmuffs.

Sumac doesn't want to be the one to hammer home that there won't be any actual bears.

"Tiddlypom," PopCorn asks Sumac, "do you not think things are icy enough on dry land?"

"You and Wood signed up for this months ago," she reminds him.

"You just want to see other people freeze so you'll feel more Christmassy," Catalpa tells Sumac.

"Not true!" Sumac turns back to PopCorn. "You've got all your sponsors already." She puts her hands on Brian's polar bear earmuffs. "The bears are counting on you . . ."

Brian does two small roars.

PopCorn looks guilty and mimes a stab wound to the heart. "Well, when you put it like that, it's hard to say no."

"So write the polar bears a check," MaxiMum stage-whispers.

"That's cheating!" Sumac points one finger at PopCorn. "What's the sticker on your bicycle? Change the something?"

Be the change you want to see in the world," he quotes.

"Well, I'm going. I know no fear," says Wood, striking a superhero pose.

"OK, OK, I surrender," says PopCorn grimly. "I'll do it."

Sumac and Brian clap.

Grumps passes through the Mess with a paper under his arm.

Sumac turns her face sideways to read the date. It's last Thursday's.

"Dad," PopCorn asks, "are you on for a swim?"

The moms exchange a dubious glance.

"What's that now?" asks Grumps.

"Jumping in the lake, for charity?"

"Oh, aye."

"Even though the water will be well below freezing, Iain?" asks MaxiMum.

The old man shrugs. "Makes no odds to me."

"If he goes into cardiac arrest, *you* explain it to the coroner," MaxiMum mutters to PopCorn.

Sumac stares: Aren't coroners for dead people?

PopCorn catches her eye. "Don't worry, pet, my dad's been leaping into icy lakes all his life."

The Lotterys are marching on the spot, sand crunching under their winter boots. Wood, PopCorn, and Grumps are the three generations of Polar Bear Plungers, and the rest are Support Team (CardaMom and Aspen to cheer them on and help them dress fast afterward, Sumac as videographer). Brian's only been persuaded to stay home on the promise of a playdate with a boy around the corner and his vast train set.

At least there's no wind on the beach right now. But tiny icebergs are bobbing on the waves of the lake. "I can't believe anyone's going to run into that water," says CardaMom with a shudder, "let alone five hundred people."

That's how many the organizers have tweeted are here. The beach is bright with Plungers in team T-shirts (Bearded Bears, The Lucky Dippers, Bear Naked Ladies) or outrageous costumes: tuxes and wedding dresses, *Sesame Street* characters, Smurfs, Elvis. . . . Two tiny kids hold up a smudged banner that says *Go Mommy*.

"Nothing like cold water for health," says Grumps, thumping his chest.

"Did you know," Sumac tells him, "a sixteen-year-old called Marilyn Bell was the first person to swim across Lake Ontario?" She points at the water, in case he doesn't remember where they are. "She had to make it fifty-two kilometers, from New York State home to Toronto, through five-meter waves, with bloodsucking lampreys biting her legs all the way!"

Grumps nods, unimpressable.

"I want a horse's head," says Aspen.

That's what's called a *non sequitur* — Latin for random. Or no, actually, Sumac sees what Aspen means now: There's a whole team of horse-headed people cantering by. "Are they really going to swim in those?"

"I wouldn't call it swimming, exactly," says PopCorn with a shudder. "You just run in, and out again right away, unless you're ultra tough. My personal goal is to stay in for a count of . . ."

"A hundred?" suggests Sumac.

"Let's say five," says PopCorn.

Aspen laughs. "You wuss!"

"Try it yourself before you start throwing insults around," suggests CardaMom.

Aspen turns back to PopCorn and bows deeply. "Sorry, oh Great Hero Father."

"That's more like it!" He shakes his fingers to warm them, looking like a clown.

Actually, PopCorn is very brave about some things, Sumac thinks — such as running into icy lakes. It's just that he's a total chicken about others, like having his teeth cleaned by the dental hygienist.

"Do you have to get your head wet for it to count?" she asks. Because that's the rule when the Lotterys compete to be First In on summertime visits to this beach. Sumac was First In twice last summer.

"No, no. Wet to the neck will count, believe me. By the way," says PopCorn, turning to Wood, "let's keep our heads dry. And remember to walk in slowly and splash your neck first before you dip — that warns your body to start tightening up blood vessels so you don't lose so much heat."

Wood nods, slapping his gloved hands together.

Her brother's being very silent: Sumac wonders if he's sick with nerves. Who wouldn't be? She's a bit nervous, and she's only the cameraperson.

Sumac's keeping the tablet insulated inside her coat so its battery won't seize up in the cold. She wonders how to get the most dramatic footage possible: Should she position herself down near the water so Wood and PopCorn and Grumps can come running past the camera into the icy waves, howling like berserkers?

"A wee dram?" asks Grumps. He's watching one team knock back shots from a tray of tiny glasses.

"We'd better not, Dad," says PopCorn. "Alcohol and subfreezing water is a dangerous combination."

The old man sniffs huffily.

"We'll get you hot chocolate from that van over there after," CardaMom promises him, "then I've prebooked a taxi straight home."

"Remember the lake we used to swim in?" Grumps throws in his son's direction.

"Do I!" says PopCorn. "Shudderingly cold in all seasons."

Soon the two of them are lost in reminiscences about Yukon.

"Were you there the time a grizzly bit him?" Aspen asks Grumps.

"Who?"

"PopCorn," says Aspen, pointing.

"Our Reginald, bitten by a bear?" Grumps asks, sarcastic. "When would this have been?"

PopCorn sounds sheepish. "Well, it sort of felt me with its teeth."

"You big old liar," says Sumac.

"It definitely sniffed me, anyway."

Aspen raps PopCorn on his wooly-hatted head. "No more big old lying."

"OK," says PopCorn. "From this day on, I will never say anything that's not a hundred and ten percent true."

"That's mathematically impossible," Sumac points out. "So you're lying again right now."

"Cross my heart," says PopCorn, doing it, "and swear —"

"He's crossing his fingers!" Aspen grabs his glove and untwists them.

"I may have been lying just now when I said I'd never lie again," says PopCorn, through snorts of laughter, "but *this* time I'm telling the absolute truth."

"You could be crossing your toes," says Sumac sternly, pointing to his boots.

CardaMom's surveying the crowd. "I bet you're the youngest here, Wood."

Sumac feels a little pang of jealousy. This is all a big thrill, but . . . everybody's going to make a massive fuss of her brother after he's Plunged, and he'll be the highlight of the Highlights Reel. She scans heads. "I wonder why there are more men than women?"

Wood shrugs. "Not really surprising."

"Why's that?" When he doesn't answer, Sumac pokes him in the arm.

"Don't make me spell it out," says Wood.

"Go ahead, son, try," says CardaMom sweetly.

"Well, guys — like, menfolk — we did evolve to be brave."

Sumac gasps in protest.

"Just physically, I mean. Come on," Wood pleads, "you know I'm right. Charging into battle and all that?"

"What about Marilyn Bell?" Sumac splutters.

"What about, uh, childbirth?" asks PopCorn.

CardaMom laughs at Wood. "He's got you there."

"Well, yeah, there's that, full marks for childbirth, ladies," says Wood. "But you notice today it's just the guys representing the Lotterys?"

"I'm just as brave as you, Mr. Manfolk," says Sumac. Anger inflates her like a balloon. "You know what? I'd do it too, easy-peasy, if I'd brought my swimsuit, and then I'd be the youngest Plunger here by *years*."

"You would so not do it," says Wood with a sly smile.

"I would so."

"Plunge in your underwear, then," he challenges her. "Nobody cares what anyone's wearing."

"Fine!"

The word's out of her mouth before Sumac realizes she has to do it now.

But she won't take it back. She's hot with wrath.

She thrusts the tablet at CardaMom. "Don't forget to keep the battery warm till you're actually filming."

"*Tsi't-ha*," begins CardaMom, "are you seriously doing this?"

"She'll wuss out at the last minute," says Aspen with a cackle.

Sumac ignores that. "And put in some dramatic close-ups, and make sure not to miss the moment we actually touch the water . . ."

"OK, Plungers!" That's the organizer through his echoey megaphone. "Are we ready?"

A wild, ragged roar answers him.

"PopCorn," Sumac calls out in a voice that's squeaky with fright, "I'm coming in too."

"Wow, for real?" PopCorn unzips his coat at top speed.

"She's bluffing." Aspen sounds uncertain now.

Sumac sheds her coat and gloves.

"Tallyho, then, prodigious progeny," PopCorn cries, beckoning her and Wood. "Time, Dad."

Grumps pulls his clothes off too, not fast, but showing no anxiety.

Clamping her teeth together so they won't chatter, Sumac whips her coat and sweater and top over her head in one go. Icy air slides under her undershirt. *Eek!* She squeals it only inside her head.

She struggles with the laces of her boots. CardaMom sets the tablet on the sand and helps her undo them.

Aspen just stares.

Sumac tugs her boots off. Her legs are bare and tingling with the startling cold. Nobody's looking at her under-wear, she reminds herself. She's fierce and fearless. *Marilyn Bell*, she chants in her mind, *Marilyn Bell, be with me now.*

The bloodsucking lampreys will be asleep in this cold, won't they?

Surely?

Sumac's hyperventilating, and she's not even in the water yet. *Deep breaths*, she tells herself, clamping her teeth together and inhaling noisily through her nose. This is going to look epic in the Highlights Reel. Sic will be so proud of his Smackeroo, doing the Plunge at only nine!

Wood is charging toward the water already, trying to get ahead of her.

"Argh!!!!" Sumac lets out a howl and speeds after him.

Her brother stops with the water at his knees: goes rigid, and hunches over. He dips his hands, and splashes his neck.

Their dad's advice was probably very sensible, but if Sumac stops now she fears she'll never get started again.

"ARGH!!" Sumac roars again, even louder, startling strangers as she lunges past them into the water.

For a second she thinks her feet have been sliced off. It's so icy, it's like kicking through metal. Sumac's in to her hips already, numb and gasping. She's way ahead of Wood — *ha, manfolk!* — and in to her chest. One more scream. *Oh my oh my oh my oh oh oh oh* . . . Sumac's jumping up and down, limbs flailing like she's been electrocuted. A splash stings her cheek. *Wet to the neck*, she thinks, *I'm wet to the neck, that counts.*

And she spins around so awkwardly she almost topples, and then lurches back out of the lake, cutting right between PopCorn and Grumps, who are wet, and blue, and splitting their sides with laughter.

It's getting dark as the taxi van brings the Lotterys home. "My feet are still killing me," Sumac

175

boasts, "and my fingers are so numb, I think I've done up my buttons wrong. But I feel fabulous!"

"Three cheers for us," crows PopCorn. "Magnificent, Dad! Bonus marks for the over-eighties."

"What's that?" says Grumps.

"You swam with icebergs," CardaMom tells him.

Grumps is looking out the window, as if he's forgotten it already.

PopCorn watches the old man, not smiling anymore.

And Sumac, watching PopCorn, thinks how strange it must be if your dad gets muddled brains, and you have to look after him, instead of vice versa, like when you were a kid.

Aspen's being remarkably quiet too. Stunned into silence by Sumac's heroisim, perhaps, thinks Sumac with a private smile.

She turns to Wood. "Let's watch the footage. I want to see the bit where you're all scaredy-cat in the shallows and I shoot right past you."

Her brother grins at that. "You mean when I get in first, super calm and cool, while you scream like a baby?"

But Sumac can't seem to find it on the tablet. She turns to CardaMom and asks, "Where's the file?"

"Oh! Yeah, that was a shame," says CardaMom.

"*What* was a shame?" demands Sumac.

"It just wouldn't turn on."

"You mean the battery seized up because you put it down on the sand and let it get cold?" Sumac's outrage swells. "I told you! And you're meant to be the techie parent!"

"Easy does it," says PopCorn.

"All she had to do was keep it warm like I said to, point the screen, and tap the red dot!"

CardaMom's face has stiffened. "I'm not liking your tone."

"Well, I'm not liking *you*." Sumac takes a long, raggedy breath.

CardaMom goes on, "I can hear that you're upset —"

"And I can see that you couldn't care less!"

"Sumac." CardaMom says it more gently than a warning. As if she's reminding Sumac who Sumac is.

But this Sumac is throbbing with rage. "So I Plunged for nothing? It was the worst cold I ever felt in my life, and I proved girls are as brave as boys, and half the family didn't see it" — her voice is getting shriller and shriller — "and I didn't even get a certificate or raise any money for the polar bears because I wasn't registered, and now there's no proof I even did it at all!"

"*A:keh!*" says CardaMom exasperatedly. "You don't need a video. You've got the memory."

Sumac feels something like a splinter of ice in her heart. She turns and stares out the window. The taxi's turning onto their street now.

Or no. Could Sumac have confused it with another one? This block's not just half dark but nearly all dark.

"Folks, this is as far as I go," says the cab driver, pulling over before the *Caution Do Not Cross* tape starts.

"Why's MaxiMum turned off all our lights?" asks Aspen, puzzled.

And Sumac sees with horror that this *is* their street. The tall white pine has dropped its huge branch between Camelottery and the Zhaos' house, ripping down two poles and all their wires.

CHAPTER 7

BITTER WEATHER

The Lotterys have had power outages before, but only quickies, not great big likely-to-last-for-days-and-weeks ones.

MaxiMum is handing out flashlights in the dark hall. "Put on more clothes, everybody — undershirts, and thick socks, and hats. Loose layers trap air better than tight ones, remember."

"Cowabunga!" That must be Opal.

"But hang on, doesn't our furnace burn natural gas?" asks Sumac.

"Yep," says MaxiMum, "but I'm afraid it still needs electricity to run. Shut the front door," she calls to Aspen.

"I'm just looking at our poor fence that got crushed by the branch," says Aspen. She's in her Moroccan woolen djellaba with the long hood up: very wizardly, especially when she puts her flashlight right under her chin to make her face eerie red.

"Maybe look out the window instead," says MaxiMum, "because every time we open an exterior door, the temperature in here falls up to five degrees."

Aspen starts closing the front door, but CardaMom pushes past her with a gigantic cooler of food from the refrigerator, saying, "Sorry, I need to put this out in the bicycle cage."

Sumac goggles at her. "Why in the cage? So burglars won't get it?"

"Raccoons," says CardaMom.

"Could we please shut that door?" pleads MaxiMum.

CardaMom does, with a thump. "Why did we get rid of all our wood-burning fireplaces?" She raps her head with her knuckles.

"Because they pollute the air," Sumac reminds her.

"Right now — who cares?" says CardaMom. "We could have been sitting around a lovely fire, toasting marshmallows . . ."

Sumac catches a glimpse of PopCorn hurrying up the stairs, his headlamp wobbling. "Can I help?" she calls.

"Sure, sweetie."

"What should I do?"

He half turns, dithering. "I don't know. Argh! Of all the times for my hubby to be away!"

"Let's fill all the baths and sinks," MaxiMum calls, "so we'll have a supply of water, and to empty the pipes before they freeze."

PopCorn points at MaxiMum. "What she said."

Sumac doesn't understand but she does it, aiming her flashlight upward and galloping past PopCorn to the third floor — bashing her ribs on the treadmill on the landing, *ouch!* — where she starts with the Rainforest.

Once they've filled the sinks and baths up and turned off the faucets, Camelottery sounds all wrong to Sumac: weirdly silent, because the furnace fans and refrigerators aren't making their usual hums and whooshes.

Luiz, in a little pool of light from a flashlight down in the Mess, is taking all this in stride. "This happens many time in my favela," he says, "especially if we are late to pay the landlord for the electricals." He's supervising a camping stove on the table that's boiling water. "A cup of tea, Mr. Grumps?" he asks as the old man wanders in.

"Don't mind if I do," says Grumps.

Luiz sounds confused. "You don't like?"

"No, he said he doesn't mind," Sumac explains. "That's Scottish for *yes please*."

Grumps sits down beside Luiz at the table. "Very dark."

"No power," Brian reminds him.

"Because another tree fell and ripped our wires down," Sumac explains.

"Ah. Mice and men," says Grumps.

"Do you mean Slate?" Sumac asks him. "Aspen's rat?"

He looks at her. "What are you blathering about now?"

"Mice and men," Sumac says. "You said —"

"The best-laid plans, I meant," says Grumps.

"Huh?" She's really confused now.

"It's from a famous poem," says CardaMom, somewhere in the dark behind her.

Drying his hands on a cloth, PopCorn adds, "Rabbie Burns, best Scottish poet ever."

"Best poet in the world," says Grumps, correcting his son.

PopCorn puts on a Scottish accent even thicker than Grumps's. *"The best laid plans o' mice an' men gang aft a-gley!"*

182

"Gang what now?" asks Catalpa.

"Often go awry," explains PopCorn. "That's the thing about plans: They generally go wrong."

"My thingummy still works all right." Grumps has taken his little radio out of his breast pocket and is fiddling with the dial.

"That's because it's got a battery," Sumac reminds him.

"Where's your fancy web now?" he says with a snort.

Sumac stares at him, thinking of spiders.

"He means the Internet," says Catalpa, wrapping one of Gram's ridiculously long scarves three times around Luiz.

Luiz laughs and tries to shove it off.

"You'll get cold," she tells him scoldingly.

Grumps has tuned his radio to a carol service. Sumac recognizes what the choir is singing. *Through the rude wind's wild lament, and the bitter weather . . .*"

It seems ages since the Lotterys were swanking around being Good Kings Wenceslas yesterday. Now it's them who've got no heat or light. More like the peasant the king sees in the woods *gathering winter fuel.*

Soon the Lotterys come together in the Mess to brainstorm about dinner. Sumac still feels deep-down chilled whenever she thinks of her Plunge; she'd love something really warming to eat. They could always boil pasta over the camping stove, but there's nothing to put on it. The freezer is full of PapaDum's chilis and stews, but without a microwave they'd take days to defrost . . .

Wood is tapping on his phone.

"Shouldn't you be saving your power for emergencies?" Sumac asks him.

"This is an emergency, numbskull."

"No, but I mean more urgent ones. Like calling an ambulance."

"What, after I defenestrate one of my sisters?"

Sumac looks around at her parents. "Did you all hear that death threat?"

"Sorry, wasn't listening. We've got two small cans of tomato soup we could heat up," offers CardaMom.

"Hate tomato," says Brian crossly.

"Does this fuel smell a bit toxic?" asks PopCorn, sniffing the air. "We could have Bits 'n' Bobs, that's always fun."

"No it's not," says Catalpa.

"How's Bits 'n' Bobs different from Deli Sandwich Delight?" Wood wants to know.

"Well . . . you don't lay everything out on the table," says PopCorn, with a toothy smile that he lights up with his flashlight. "People just help themselves to whatever wild combo they fancy from the fridge. Or in this case, from the bicycle cage."

"So, just to be clear, it's a Lazy Dad's Deli Sandwich Delight?" says Catalpa.

Last time they had Bits 'n' Bobs, Sumac ended up with a chunk of some hard cheese that'd lost its wrapper, half a persimmon, and some stale walnuts. Her mind boggles at what she'd get tonight, working by flashlight in the bike cage: marmalade on salami, probably. "I Plunged today in my *underwear*," she says in a voice that comes out choked, "and nobody seems to care, and —"

"Of course we do," says MaxiMum. "Well done, you."

What an anticlimax.

"My point is, now I want a hot dinner!" says Sumac.

"We'd all like that," says MaxiMum, in her irritatingly calm voice.

"Score!" Wood looks up from his phone.

"Nobody cares if you've leveled up or won some virtual gems," Catalpa tells him scathingly.

"Do you care that I've got us invited around to the Roses'?" asks Wood smugly.

"What do you mean, *got* us invited?" MaxiMum sounds wary. "You do *not* text friends asking if your party of eleven can pop around for a hot dinner."

"I wouldn't! I just mentioned our power outage in a jokey kind of way, and Baruch texted back" — he reads it aloud from his screen — "*Dad sez made waaaaay 2 many latkes so come on down.*"

"I stay here," says Luiz quickly. "Your friends don't know me."

"Leave you alone in a cold, dark house?" says Catalpa. "Don't be ridiculous."

✻

"*Ajo!*" says CardaMom with a gasp as they step out into the icy night. Even Wood's wearing full-length jeans and gloves, because it's what he calls *wicked cold.*

The Lotterys pick their way down the street, swinging their beams of light to make sure they don't walk into any pointy fallen branches. "Latkes are crispy potato pancakes," Sumac tells Grumps.

"Had pancakes already," says Grumps.

Sumac's impressed he remembers. "That was breakfast, and these are a special Jewish kind."

Catalpa is gripping Luiz's elbow and nagging him to keep his head down so his bubble will stay in the right place.

The wind is nipping Sumac's earlobes at the bottom of her hat. "Good King Wenceslas" is an earworm stuck in her head: *Through the rude wind's wild lament, and the bitter weather.* It occurs to her that when things get *weathered*, it means damaged, because the wind or the rain or the snow

186

or the sun have worn them down, stained the wood, or cracked the rock. You can even have a *weather-beaten* face. Maybe everybody looks like a crumbly old rock by the time they get to Grumps's age. Sumac feels her own round, numb cheeks, and is glad she's still only nine.

The Roses are the kind of tidy small family (just the boys and their dad — their mom lives in Florida) that Sumac loves to visit. She fantasizes about having just one or two parents and siblings, and a small, quiet house, where everybody knows where their shoes are.

Baruch and Ben and their dad, Mark, hurry to carry lots of folding chairs up from the basement for the Lotterys, and somehow squeeze them all into their living room. For Luiz they've got their antique school desk, with a pile of cushions on the flat bit for him to lean his face on.

There's a beautiful silver candelabra standing in the window with three blue and three white candles burning. "We could see this from right down the street. It's nice you don't shut your curtains," says Sumac.

"That'd be against the rules," Ben tells her, grinning. "Hanukkah — the Festival of Lights — is about remembering a war fought for religious freedom, so displaying the *chanukiah* is kind of the whole point." (Ben's a know-it-all to match Sic. They met when they were finalists in a local Championship of Nerds.)

"Where are the other three candles?" Catalpa asks, looking at the empty branches.

"We'll put them in over the next three evenings," Mark explains. "We're only five days into Hanukkah — it's one more candle each night."

"No touching," Brian reminds herself in a whisper, standing very close to the candles.

"But I count six burning, not five." Sumac tallies them again, to be sure.

"Well spotted," says Mark. "The upper one's the *shamash* — the word means servant, or helper — the special candle you use to light all the others."

"Hanukkah lasts eight days because that's how long the rebels' menorah kept burning even though it only had a teensy amount of oil in it," says Ben.

CardaMom goes over to the sideboard to help herself to another two latkes with applesauce, and lets out a groan of pleasure. "I'm so glad you didn't make them with grated sweet potatoes instead of regular potatoes, Mark."

"Yeah, we outvoted him at the last minute," says Baruch.

"Good call. Holiday food shouldn't be healthy," says PopCorn, reaching for

another three and dolloping on sour cream, with a sprinkle of green onions.

Sumac is busy trying out different latke toppings: smoked salmon, figs, Greek yogurt, and pomegranate seeds. But after that she goes back to good old applesauce.

The Roses pay attention properly when Sumac tells them about her Plunge. Well, hers and Wood's and PopCorn's and Grumps's — the old man even put his whole head under the water! But Sumac was the youngest Plunger by far, and she might get her name in the newspaper, even if they'll probably spell it wrong.

She doesn't mention about CardaMom letting the tablet freeze up, because she's feeling a bit ashamed of her tantrum in the taxi: not her maturest moment ever.

Mark pours wine for the six adults and lifts his glass. *"L'chaim tovim ul'shalom!* To good life and peace."

"L'chaim!" The kids lift their juice glasses and join in the toast, though Sumac's not sure she's saying it right.

"What do Brazilians say for cheers?" she asks Luiz.

"Como?"

She clinks her glass against his. "Cheers!"

"Ah yes. *Saúde!* For the health." Luiz drinks.

"Like *santé* in French," says CardaMom.

Luiz has thought of another. *"Tim-Tim!"*

"Ah, like our *chin-chin*," says PopCorn.

"Ours?" CardaMom says mockingly. "I think we borrowed it from Italian."

"*Sláinte*," says Grumps, waving his glass so the little bit of wine sloshes nearly over the edge.

"Now, who's ready to play dreidel?" asks Baruch.

"Bring it," says Wood in a pretend-villain snarl, rolling up his sleeves.

Wood's played it before, but the rest of the Lotterys haven't. The dreidel's a spinning top with a Hebrew letter on each of its four sides. If you throw a *shin*, that means you put one coin in the pot. *Nun* means you pass to the next player, *hay* means you take half of what's in the pot, and *gimel* means you get all of it.

They start with fifteen coins each (the gold ones are milk chocolate, the silver ones dark). But soon Sumac's down to six.

Ben comforts her: "The score doesn't really matter, anyway, because the game was played as a cover for studying."

Wood mimes horror. "I've been suckered into studying?"

"Back in the day — the Maccabean Revolt against the Seleucid Empire, this was —"

"That sounds so *Star Wars*," says Aspen.

"Yeah, except about two thousand years ago. Anyway,

the Jews gathered in caves to study the Torah, which was forbidden by the Greek king," says Ben, "and if the lookout spotted soldiers coming, the Jews would hide their scrolls and spin the dreidel so it looked like they were just gambling."

"Crafty," says Sumac.

"So, the opposite of when you tell the parents you're going on an algebra site and actually you're watching Nerf gun battles," Catalpa says to Wood.

CardaMom's eyebrows soar.

"In other words, studying ballistics and strategy," Wood corrects his sister, poker-faced.

It only takes half an hour for Sumac to lose all her coins (though she's pretty sure Brian's eaten a few of them).

Walking the few blocks home from the Roses' house, Sumac still feels full, but the warmth soon wears off.

"Bad news," says PopCorn, stopping so suddenly that Aspen crashes into him from behind. He holds up his phone.

Sumac peers at it and reads it aloud: "*All Fights Canceled.* But that's lovely. Is it a global cease-fire?" she asks. Like the Christmas Day in World War I when the soldiers on both sides stopped shooting and sang carols . . .

"Are you drunk?" Wood asks Sumac.

"*Flights*, with an *l*," says PopCorn. "All flights canceled. Nothing's coming in or out of Toronto, because of the ice."

"But PapaDum and Sic's plane will be stuck in midair," Sumac wails. "What if it runs out of fuel and drops out of the sky?"

Brian bursts into tears.

"Would everyone kindly calm down?" asks MaxiMum.

"PapaDum sent a message I've only just got, to say they were turned back to land again at Delhi," says PopCorn.

Dilli abhi door hai, Sumac remembers. She shouldn't have counted her chickens, because Delhi's *still* very far away.

"It's OK, *tsi't-ha*," CardaMom tells Brian, wrapping her up in an awkward hug on the slippery sidewalk. "They're perfectly safe, they just won't be home for Christmas."

"Want them safe *here*," shrieks Brian, and she sobs on.

Sumac wishes she could cry too; wishes she was four instead of nine. She swallows hard. "Well, at least they'll have heat and light and stuff at the hostel, not like the rest of us," she says in a wavering voice. She meant that PapaDum and Sic would be all right . . . but it came out like self-pity about the power outage.

"I know things are a bit ridiculous at the moment, kids, but we just have to weather it," says CardaMom.

"*Weather* we like it or not!" That's Aspen.

They all groan at the pun, but actually it does make Sumac feel ever so slightly better.

They shuffle on down the sidewalk toward their dark house. "When I was giving birth to you, Catalpa, you know what the midwife told me was the most important muscle?" asks CardaMom.

"You are so random, Mother," says Catalpa.

Squeamish, Sumac tries to remember the names of any muscles in her lower half. "The abs?"

"Don't think I really want to hear this," mutters Wood, plugging his ears.

"The muscle of surrender," says CardaMom.

"That's not actually a thing," says MaxiMum scientifically.

"Where's the muscle of surrender?" asks Sumac, bewildered.

CardaMom taps her own head. "Let go, relax, let things happen as they will."

Oh, a metaphorical muscle.

"I'd be good at surrendering," says PopCorn, a little more cheerfully.

"I got muscles," Brian informs her family, making a duck with her short right arm.

"When I was having the boys, I found that pushing really hard worked well," says MaxiMum with a small grin.

Yeah, Sumac would say she's more the pushing than the surrendering sort, herself.

She sets her teeth together and tries out a grin in the dark. *Pull yourself together*, she tells herself. The parents have the tricky job of getting the family right through the holidays without PapaDum *or* electricity. Sumac prides herself on being the most responsible kid, doesn't she? (Like the special helper candle, she remembers: the *shamash*.) It's OK that these holidays are messed up a certain amount — just like the Leaning Tower of Pisa, which tilts four degrees all the time, without ever falling down. Surely if Sumac really, really tries, she can still get into the festive spirit?

It's a long night at Camelottery.

Sumac gets to sleep easily enough, but she's woken at one in the morning by terrible sounds. "I heard three separate pops — bangs, really. Like guns or something!" she tells PopCorn on the third-floor landing.

"I know," he says, sounding unnerved. "Fireworks, maybe?"

"But who'd be setting off fireworks?"

The painted-like-ancient-wood door to Catalpa's Turret crashes open. She's wearing a fake fur sweater, a robe, and a hunter's cap with earflaps. "Would you guys please keep the yapping down? You'll wake poor Luiz."

"All the way down in the basement?" says PopCorn, unconvinced.

"There were three deafening bangs," Sumac tells Catalpa in a whisper.

"So what?"

"If only PapaDum were here, he'd know if the house was about to explode," mutters PopCorn, chewing his thumb.

"Explode?" echoes Sumac in a squeal.

Wood flings open his door, wearing only a T-shirt and pajama bottoms, and directs his flashlight beam from face to face as if he's hunting runaway prisoners. "They're called frost quakes. I *told* you all about them. The frozen ground expands and cracks."

"You regurgitate so much boring weather stuff, you can't possibly expect us to take in more than a small percentage," says Catalpa, and thumps her door shut.

Then Aspen emerges from her Asp Pit and says she's bored and can she watch something.

"Power outage, remember?" says Sumac.

"On the tablet, then," says Aspen.

"Well . . ." PopCorn says in his about-to-cave voice.

MaxiMum comes up from the landing below, yawning. "We're *not* going to use up our batteries watching movies in the night," she tells Aspen. "I suggest you read under the covers with a flashlight, like kids have done ever since the invention of flashlights."

"When was that?" Sumac wants to know.

"I refuse to homeschool anyone at" — MaxiMum checks her watch — "nearly two in the morning. Let's all go back to sleep."

Aspen insists on coming upstairs with Sumac and sharing her bed *to keep warm*, which in practice means singing annoying songs like "Ninety-Nine Bottles of Beer on the Wall" to pass the time . . . so Sumac doesn't get to sleep again till after three.

Now it's morning and the sun's up, at least, though it's not making Camelottery any warmer. Sumac sits curled up with her duvet all around her so she's shaped like an ice-cream cone (and her nose is as cold as one), reading. That's usually the best medicine.

She's trying to find that wonderful Christmas scene in *Little House on the Prairie*, but she keeps coming across racist remarks about *savages*, so she gives up.

Christmas Eve today. The Lotterys always do Kris Kringle, giving each other their handmade gifts . . . but Sumac doubts anybody will be in the mood.

She heads downstairs to find some breakfast, at least.

Oak, in the doorway of the little kids' room, pulls himself to standing on the doorframe. He's got diaper cream drawn across both cheeks like a football player, and all he's wearing is sweatpants, but he shows no sign of feeling the chill. He sways forward as if he's going to take a step . . . but maybe Sumac's just imagining that.

She smiles at Oak, because she can't not; he always cheers her up. "Did you paint yourself again, Michelangelo?" she asks him, extricating his sticky fingers from the door hinge before they get pinched.

Brian runs out triumphantly to greet Sumac. "I swallowed a marble!"

Sumac stares at her. "Are you kidding?"

"Afraid not," says CardaMom, coming out with a cloth to wipe Oak's cheeks.

It's usually Aspen who swallows foreign objects. "What did you do that for?" Sumac asks Brian.

"I keeping Oak safe."

Sumac frowns. "You were keeping the marble away from him?"

Brian nods. "In my mouth. So he don't see."

Sumac can see a certain logic in that. "I still don't get how you swallowed it."

"Oaky made me laugh lots."

"Still —"

"They were lying on their backs at the time, playing Starfish, so it fell down Brian's throat," CardaMom explains. Sounding way too relaxed, in Sumac's opinion.

"Shouldn't we be bringing her to the hospital?" Sumac whispers it in her mom's ear, so Brian won't panic.

CardaMom shakes her head. "We've decided to let nature take its course."

"What does that mean?"

"Watch and wait," says CardaMom.

"We poke all my poops with a fork," says Brian gleefully, "till we find Mr. Marble."

Sumac feels sick. "I don't think I ever want to be a parent," she says to CardaMom.

CardaMom lets out a whoop of laughter and says, "You get used to the icky stuff."

In the Hall of Mirrors, Sumac finds Luiz stroking one of the red furry stockings hanging from the coatrack behind the tree. Each has a tiny drawing of one of the Lotterys dangling from it. PopCorn's even done one for Luiz, showing him with one eye patched.

"They'll get magically filled with presents tonight," Sumac explains, doing air quotes around *magically* so he won't think she's a baby.

One of the Lotterys has remembered to put a mince pie and a tot of whiskey out for Santa already, with carrots for the reindeer. That makes Sumac feel a tiny bit more Christmassy.

"In Brazil," says Luiz, "we put the socks on our — on the shelf under the window."

"Windowsill," says Sumac.

"The clean socks, you understand, not dirty."

She grins. "They do socks in the Philippines too — where my birth mom is from."

"A lump of coal, you get, if you're naughty," says Grumps, passing through the hall with what looks like three sweaters on, and a mug in each hand.

"Not nowadays," Sumac tells him. "Kids get presents whether we're naughty or not."

Grumps sniffs. "That's the problem!"

"Fleeting, sprogs," comes a roar from the Mess: PopCorn. "Come all ye to the Fleeting."

Family meetings are called that because (a) if you say *family meeting* really fast it sounds quite like *fleeting*, and (b) *fleeting* means quick, which is what the Lotterys prefer meetings to be.

All of them turn up to this one except Grumps (because he never really follows what's being argued about anyway). Today's topic is:

TO STAY OR GO?

"Really, I think we're better off here," says CardaMom, "at least for the first couple of nights, while the house still has some residual heat."

Sumac's stomach sinks. How long could this power outage possibly last? While it was only happening to other people on the street — in fact, all over Toronto — well, in fact, all the way from Oklahoma to Newfoundland — it seemed like a minor problem. (She's embarrassed by that now; she realizes it wasn't one bit minor to the other people.) But when it happens to *your* family, on Christmas Eve, it feels like a total disaster.

Her hands are cold and they're only going to get colder. She puts them in her pockets and grips the furry fabric miserably.

"My nose be running," says Brian, and wipes it on her sleeve.

"We could make a festive camp in the Gym-Jo," suggests CardaMom.

"Why the Gym-Jo?" asks Sumac.

"Yeah," says Wood, "doesn't heat rise — so shouldn't the attic be the warmest level?"

"If the furnace were on, yeah," says MaxiMum. "But what we need now is insulation, and the basement is insulated by the ground, so it should stay warmer than the outside air, especially if we cover the windows with bubble wrap."

"I refuse to sleep in the Gym-Jo with you lot," says Catalpa stonily.

"Oh, believe me, the feeling is mutual," says Wood. "I'd rather make myself a shelter of branches in the Ravine."

"You're such a poseur," Catalpa tells him, then turns back toward their parents. "May I ask, why can't we all go to a hotel?"

Wood sneers, "Listen to Princess!"

Catalpa tries to slap him, but he ducks away.

"No hitting," says Brian, and lifts her hand to smack Catalpa's knee . . .

But CardaMom catches hold of Brian's fingers just in time. "No hitting by *anyone.*"

"Actually, I tried to book us hotel rooms first thing this morning," admits MaxiMum, "but they're all gone."

Kind of like Mary and Joseph, Sumac thinks: no room at the inn.

"Dada Ji and Dadi Ji?" suggests MaxiMum.

Those are PapaDum's dad and mom, who live in a suburb of Toronto.

"Realistically," PopCorn begins — which is a strange way for this particular parent to start a sentence, Sumac thinks — "realistically, we can't have more than a few of us barge in on them."

"But that wouldn't be fair," says Sumac. "How would we pick who'd get to be all warm and cozy and watching movies in their house?"

"Luiz, obviously, duh, because he's our guest," says Catalpa. "And I'm looking after him."

Aspen meets Sumac's eyes and smirks; Catalpa will clearly use any excuse to get into their grandparents' comfy house.

"But the ones who'll feel the cold most are the youngest and the oldest," says MaxiMum, "so logically it should be Oak, Brian, and Grumps —"

"Grumps can't look after Brian and Oak," protests CardaMom.

"As I would have said if you'd let me finish my sentence." MaxiMum almost sounds tetchy. "So a parent should go with Grumps and . . . just Oak, maybe, not Brian?"

"*I* go with Oaky always," roars Brian.

"If Grumps is hardy enough for the Polar Bear Plunge, I think the old dude could handle sleeping in an unheated house," mutters Aspen.

"Fine! On your head be it if your grandfather dies of hyperthermia in the night," Catalpa tells her.

"Melodrama is unhelpful," MaxiMum tells Catalpa. "And heat stroke seems unlikely right now, so I think the word you're looking for is hy*po*thermia."

Catalpa shows her teeth in a silent snarl.

"*Or,*" says MaxiMum, "we could all walk over to the nearest Warming Center."

"Is that like a big lodge with crackling log fires?" Aspen wants to know.

Wood laughs at that.

"Ah, not exactly," says MaxiMum, "but it will have heat, light, and even Wi-Fi."

"That's if it's not already crammed with folks who've already been without power for forty-eight hours," mutters CardaMom. "I still vote for Camelottery."

"Let's divide up, then," says MaxiMum with a shrug. "PopCorn, why don't you get a taxi out to PapaDum's folks with Oak, Brian, and Grumps?"

"And don't forget to poke Brian's poop," CardaMom tells him.

PopCorn looks aghast.

"Oh, didn't you tell him the marble story yet?" she asks Brian.

"Wood," asks MaxiMum, "are you on for toughing it out here with CardaMom?"

"Need you ask?" Wood straightens up. "I'm going to cook us up a lot of pig on the barbecue in the Wild."

"Which leaves me, Sumac, and Aspen to try our luck at the Warming Center," says MaxiMum.

"Hello?" complains Catalpa. "What about Luiz and me — don't we exist?"

"Whoops," MaxiMum admits, "I lost count."

Luiz stands in the door of the Mess, his face so stricken that Sumac thinks his eyeball must have suddenly ripped again.

"Lotterys," he says, "*desculpe*, I am so sorry to make so very lot of trouble."

"What is it, Luiz?" asks PopCorn, jumping up.

"No no, the same old. Here you are all worry where to go, and I am one more problem."

"Not at all," says CardaMom, grinning. "This family is so big anyway, you're just a drop in the ocean."

"You are kind," Luiz tells her.

"The Greeks said you had to," says Sumac.

Everybody looks at her. "Do good guest-friendship, I

mean, or you'd be smited," she says awkwardly. "They had a special word for it I can't remember." *Xena*, like the Warrior Princess?

Luiz says to the parents, "I will stay here, yes? A cold house is very OK with me."

"But you're recovering from an operation," MaxiMum protests.

"I'm not sick," Luiz insists, "I only have to keep my bubble where the doctor say." He taps above his eye.

"If you're staying at Camelottery, I suppose I'll have to as well," Catalpa tells him with a discontented sigh.

"No no!" Luiz waves his hands at her. "My accidental was only my fault. No more to blame Catalpa," he tells the whole group. "I'm a man" — he thumps his chest — "and she is a child. What kind of fool am I think, to grab moving cars and sled behind?"

"I'm *fourteen*," says Catalpa, outraged, "and I'm staying with you."

So it seems to be settled.

As Sumac steps out into the Hall of Mirrors, she spots Grumps putting Santa's whole mince pie into his mouth. "Oh, but —"

She stops herself before she can say, *None of that's for you.*

Now Grumps picks up the little tot glass, and washes his pie down with whiskey.

Well, she decides, he is the only old man in the house: Maybe she should think of him like Santa in disguise, like Zeus and Hermes were disguised in the Greek myth. "Is the mince pie good?"

"Capital," Grumps murmurs indistinctly. "My mammy's were always the best."

Does he mean this one tastes like his mammy's, or does he think she made it? Never mind, Sumac tells herself.

Sumac looks around the Warming Center, trying to keep her face from showing what she's thinking, in case one of the Red Cross volunteers decides she's ungrateful.

There's a tiny artificial Christmas tree in one corner of the huge hall, with three strands of red tinsel wound around it. The army cots are all taken already, so the three Lotterys each get a mat on the floor, a thin pillow, and a thin crinkly blanket stamped *Emergency*.

"Like some smelly school gym," says Aspen.

"Shush," Sumac hisses in her ear. "Some people sleep in shelters all the time. Or under bridges."

"Too true," murmurs MaxiMum, setting down her bag.

Sumac's shoulder is sore from carrying hers, because she had to pack so fast that she couldn't decide between *Greek*

206

Myths, *Little Women*, *Tuck Everlasting*, and her beloved hardback of *Grimms' Fairy Tales* — so she brought them all.

Adults and teenagers cluster around four points on the walls. Oh, those must be the charging outlets, Sumac realizes. People are lining up with their devices like they're horses drinking from a pond of electricity.

Aspen scampers back from the tables at the end of the hall, her arms loaded. A protein bar drops to the floor, and then a bottle of water, then a toiletries kit. "Look what I scored!"

"That's food for people who need it," Sumac points out, "whereas we had BLTs and curly fries on the way here."

Aspen scowls and goes back to shed her load. She's not even hungry for any of it — she just loves freebies.

MaxiMum gets herself a coffee from the big urn, then answers a ping on her phone, and tells the girls she's going to meditate.

"What, right now, right here?" complains Sumac, feeling shy.

"I need it," says MaxiMum with a shrug. "Ever wondered why I've ended up a Buddhist?"

"Uh . . . because you're, I don't know, more serene and enlightened than the rest of us?"

MaxiMum lets out a guffaw. "If I seem that way, it's the

effect of meditating, not the cause. A radiant personality like CardaMom can sail through life on sheer warmth, whereas me . . . if I didn't have my practice, I just might slaughter you all."

"Wow," says Aspen, big-eyed.

"OK, go meditate then," says Sumac hurriedly.

MaxiMum kneels down on her mat and shuts her eyes.

Actually, Sumac needn't have worried about people thinking her mother's weird, because some of them are doing even odder things. She sees one woman curling her eyelashes with scary tongs. Another doing some yoga exercise where you sit cross-legged and hoist yourself into the air on your two hands. One quite big kid picking his nose. A man is ranting into his phone about his car getting *totaled* and how it wasn't his fault, and he has no idea where he's left his medication. Basically everybody's pretending their mat or cot is a tiny bedroom they're alone in, Sumac realizes.

There are lots of old people playing cards. Or doing sudoku or crosswords, which reminds Sumac of Grumps. It's weird to have the family be in four different places (counting Delhi) on Christmas Eve. She lays out her four books beside her mat, to make it a bit homier.

"A computer down in that corner's playing *Frozen* for the little kids, but I don't think I can bear to watch it one

208

more time," Aspen reports. "And there's a guitar anyone can use, apparently, and a piano . . ."

"Don't do your plonky pretend playing," Sumac begs her. "You'll get us kicked out."

Aspen stalks off, head in the air, and a few minutes later Sumac sees her playing Pictionary with three bigger kids.

Sumac lies on her mat, trying to find the best position. But every time she gets comfy, the light's in the wrong place for reading her *Greek Myths*. So she sits up. Sleeping on a hard floor can't be half as bad as being chained to a rock like Prometheus and having her liver torn out by an eagle, she reminds herself.

Hey, somebody's brought a Labradoodle puppy, so Sumac goes over to stroke it for a while. Two cats in carriers are hissing at each other; one of their owners ends up having to swap mats with someone on the other side of the hall. Also a pair of baby twins — almost as cute as the Labradoodle.

Sumac misses Oak, and hopes Dadi Ji and Dada Ji are giving him a lovely bath in their whirlpool tub. As for Grumps, he probably won't have any idea where he is . . .

"There's a turtle and a parakeet," Aspen comes back to tell MaxiMum, "and you made me leave Slate to suffer at home!"

"Well, rats have a tendency to make people scream," MaxiMum reminds her. "I'm sure he'll be fine. Don't his cousins survive in the sewers all winter?"

Sumac wonders how cold it's gotten at Camelottery now, and whether the others are having more fun than her.

She and MaxiMum get talking to a woman who's already spent two nights in this Warming Center with her dad. He's in a wheelchair because he can't move from the neck down. She had to call the police to carry him out of their third-floor apartment since the elevator wasn't working. "The tree came right through my window while I was sleeping, and all I got was a scratch," says the woman, showing a bandage on her cheek. "So lucky!"

MaxiMum says the three of them don't have to sit around in the Warming Center all afternoon. So they go rent skates at the local outdoor rink — getting hot chocolate to keep warm.

And then, wonder of wonders, they pass a sign outside a church that says:

THE SOUND OF MUSIC SHOWING 3 PM
ALL WELCOME to SING ALONG!

MaxiMum calls CardaMom to see if she and the others want to come. But apparently she and Wood are doing a big hike in the Ravine, and Catalpa's staying home with Luiz to paint his nails ten different colors.

Sumac's favorite song in the movie is "My Favorite Things." While she waits for it, she's suffering through "Sixteen Going on Seventeen" — the drippy one about Liesl and Rolf being in love — when suddenly she gets hit by a thought. Literally hit: like a kick to her chest.

Catalpa's got a crush on Luiz!

A *massive* one.

She must have. It makes sense of her insisting on "nursing" him all the time (when Luiz is perfectly able to lean forward without help), and going to all that trouble to make things for him to sleep on or look into — even figuring out the angles for that mirror, when geometry is *not* her strong suit. With her scornful face, and complaints about being stuck with their couchsurfer, Catalpa fooled them all. Yeah, maybe she really did find Luiz annoying at the start of his visit, Sumac decides, but now she laughs at his jokes and winds scarves around his neck to keep him cozy. What else could that mean but lurrrrrve?

There's a five-year gap between fourteen and nineteen, which must be embarrassingly huge when you're fourteen.

Sumac turns to Aspen in the darkened cinema to whisper what she's just figured out . . .

And then she thinks better of it. Aspen's such a blabbermouth, she'll never be able to keep it to herself, and next thing, all the sibs will be teasing Catalpa about her crush. Which would actually be cruel, Sumac realizes — a gigantic, stinky antipresent for Christmas.

Also, Luiz would be sure to hear about it, and it would make the rest of his stay pretty awkward.

So Sumac presses her lips together, and zips them, and locks them. Though she doesn't throw away the imaginary key, she pockets it. Because she's going to save the secret to use as a weapon the next time Catalpa's being really vile to her.

Back at the Warming Center, the three Lotterys are just in time for dinner.

The food's surprisingly good, actually: pasta and garlic bread and Caesar salad and pecan pie, all served up by the Red Cross volunteers. "It's nice of you to spend your Christmas Eve feeding us," Sumac tells one older woman.

The woman gives her a tired pat on the shoulder and says, "Well, there's only me at home, so I like the company."

There's Harry No Name in the line for pie. "Harry!" Aspen throws her arms around their neighbor, startling him.

"Lotterys! How's it hanging?" asks Harry. "What have you done with the rest of yourselves?"

Sumac and Aspen — speaking at the same time — explain their complicated arrangements.

"You two got the best of it," Harry tells them, gesturing around. "This place is a much sweeter deal than the shelter I used to crash at. Chocolate pretzels, and pets, even."

"I know!" Aspen scowls. "We could have brought our parrot and cats and dog and my lovely rat, instead of leaving them all to freeze their little butts off at home . . ."

After dinner, Harry teaches the Lotterys a kind of poker called Five-Card Draw — they bet with pretzels — and MaxiMum, no surprise, turns out to have an excellent poker face.

Then she lets Sumac and Aspen watch *Pitch Perfect* on the tablet, sharing a pair of earphones. But half an hour in, Sumac is yawning. She'd forgotten she missed so much sleep last night because of frost quakes and "Ninety-Nine Bottles."

She stretches out on her mat and tucks the emergency blanket around her. "The lights are too bright," she complains.

MaxiMum dangles an airline sleep mask over her.

"Good packing," says Sumac, grabbing it.

"Why don't I get one?" complains Aspen.

MaxiMum takes out a second mask, pulls back the elastic, and slingshots it at Aspen, so it lands on her head. "Earplugs, anyone?"

"Yes!"

"Yes!"

Sumac lies on her side with the mask fitted over her eyes and works on ignoring all the noise going on around her. At least it's warm, she tells herself. She tries to imagine living on your own, like that volunteer woman. A family of one. She supposes you'd get some peace and quiet, anyway . . .

CHAPTER 8
- - - - - - - - - - - - - - - - - - - -
AMIGO SECRETO

It's still dark: 7:37 AM by Sumac's watch. That's how you know you're not a little kid anymore — you don't wake yourself up with excitement at five on Christmas Morning.

Little noises all around her in the Warming Center: a stranger's snore, and the little tinny sound of someone listening to music on earbuds. Somebody — or more than one somebody — has farted in their sleep.

Also, Sumac feels as if she's been beaten up in the night. This mat sucks.

She leans up on her elbows to peer out the nearest window of the hall. Down a little slit between skyscrapers to the east, the sun is about to rise. *Come on*, Sumac whispers to the tiny sliver of yellow light, *you can do it . . .*

A brutal thump, and she's pinned to the floor, face-down. Like being attacked by a flying monkey from *The Wizard of Oz*. It's Aspen: "Happy Christmas!"

"Get *off* me."

Aspen kisses her ear. "Sumac the Grinchy Scrooge!"

"I am not," Sumac groans. "I just — you're crushing me to death!"

"Shh," whispers MaxiMum, flat on her back on her mat beside them. "Happy Christmas. Remember how to whisper?"

"I am whispering," Aspen assures her in her regular voice.

Sumac heaves her sister off her, then gives her one smacky kiss.

In the line for breakfast (scrambled eggs and sausage patties), MaxiMum stretches her arms high over her head and says, "These old bones . . ."

"Where?" asks Aspen, peering at her plate.

"My bones," says MaxiMum, rubbing her hip. "I think I'd rather sleep in my own cold bed than another night on this floor."

"Me too," Sumac tells her eagerly. "And it's been fun and all, trying out the Warming Center, but I miss the rest of our gang."

"CardaMom says it's actually not that bad in the house if they keep moving," says MaxiMum, reading her phone.

"So can we?" Sumac asks her.

"Can we what?" asks Aspen, who's lost the thread of the conversation.

"Go home for Christmas!" Sumac tells her.

Camelottery's pretty icy: You can see your breath on the air. But it's a thrill to be home swapping big hugs and stories of last night with CardaMom, Wood, Catalpa, and Luiz. Then PopCorn, Grumps, and the smalls turn up too, "to give PapaDum's folks a bit of a break from us today," says PopCorn.

"You mean you've all been driving them up the wall?" asks CardaMom.

Sumac does that thing where she puts Oak's entire plump foot in her mouth to make him howl with laughter.

"*Feliz Natal*," Luiz keeps saying, giving everyone two cheek kisses.

"Fleece what?" says Brian.

"It means like your Happy Christmas," he tells her.

"I did three poops in Dadi Ji's toilet," Brian tells him, "and we poked them with a plastic fork, but we don't find my marble."

Sumac prods her in the belly. "Come on, Mr. Marble!"

Brian finds this hilarious and keeps pressing her finger into different spots. "Come on, Mr. Marble!"

"I know what, I'm going to have my self-heating meal," says Aspen, while the others are putting together boring bread and cheese from the bicycle cage.

"Great idea," says CardaMom.

"You know you're basically congratulating her on stealing from the hungry?" asks Sumac.

CardaMom shrugs resignedly, mouth full of Brie.

Aspen does something Sumac's never known her to do: read the instructions before she begins. She puts the pouch of boneless pork rib inside the heater bag on top of the pad, pours the tiny tube of salt water into the bag (where it's going to react with an alloy of magnesium and iron, apparently), folds and stickers it shut, and slides it all back in the box. "Oo, it'll be hot and delicious, you guys are going to be so jealous!"

Persuading a meal to self-heat takes twelve minutes. Aspen hovers in the Mess watching the timer count down on PopCorn's phone, and irritating the other Lotterys by demonstrating how flexible her joints are.

"*Such* a show-off," mutters Wood.

"In Brazil we say" — Luiz strikes a red-carpet pose — "you put a watermelon on your head."

Aspen snorts with amusement. "But what if the person was showing off by putting an actual watermelon on their head?"

"Don't even think about it." CardaMom points a finger at her. "We're still finding sticky traces of the melon Brian dropped a few days ago."

"It dropped itself!" Brian tries to smack CardaMom.

Who steps deftly out of the way and says, "Gentle hands, *tsi't-ha*, or you'll go outside the room."

Eyes narrowed, Brian weighs up the risk. Then puts her hands in her pockets and snarls, "They be gentle."

Wood challenges Luiz to a thumb-wrestling match that makes both of them snigger a lot. Wood wins, but Sumac suspects Luiz has let him.

Ping: Aspen's twelve minutes are up. She rips her pouch open, pours it into the tray, tries a big forkful, and . . .

"Yeuch!" She runs to spit it into the sink.

This makes her siblings laugh a lot.

"That's the nastiest thing I've ever put in my mouth."

"Says the girl who chews her own braids," murmurs CardaMom.

"And toenails," says Wood.

Aspen protests. "I never!"

"I even caught it on video a while back," Wood tells her.

It occurs to Sumac that maybe the Lotterys weren't really doing all those power-less neighbors a favor the other morning, by handing out pouch meals that taste so vile. Hopefully the sandwiches were better?

A whoosh of water from the Can-Do (their ground-floor washroom) on the other side of the wall. "Only flush if you *really* need to, remember?" CardaMom calls. "Because the water's not going to last."

"This is getting squalid already," mutters MaxiMum.

Sumac wants something Christmassy to happen. "Can we open our stockings now?"

"I forgot all about them!" Aspen runs into the hall to scoop them all up.

Sumac gets . . . a clip-on book light, soft aloe socks, and a chocolate orange. Nice, though none of it wows her, exactly.

The best present is probably the soft leather penguin shoes for Oak, which light up every time he moves his feet.

"How would you be spending the day back in Brazil?" Catalpa asks Luiz.

"To the beach," he tells her.

She groans. "That sounds fantastic!"

"Prawns on the barbie," remarks Grumps.

Sumac wonders what he means.

"And pavlova for afters," Grumps goes on. "Elspeth took her tights off."

That's PopCorn's dead mom.

"Was this . . . back in Glasgow?" asks Wood.

Grumps snorts at the idea. "New Zealand! Barbecue at the beach, 1966," he says, tapping his head in triumph because he's remembered the year.

"That was the time we spent Christmas with Aunt Patricia — your sister?" asks PopCorn.

Grumps nods. "Blistering sunshine in December, on account of the world being upside down."

Sumac frowns, then figures out that Grumps means New Zealanders — in the Southern Hemisphere — have their summer during the Northern Hemisphere's winter.

Grumps points one flat finger at PopCorn: "You burned your wee bum off."

The kids hoot with laughter at the image.

"Because I was crawling around — smaller than Oak," PopCorn protests, "and the Scots don't believe in sunblock."

Sumac would hate it to be hot in December, actually; totally unseasonal. Even worse than freezing rain. "Can we do Kris Kringle now?"

Catalpa explains the ritual to Luiz.

"Ah, we do this in Brazil too," he says, "but we call it *amigo secreto*."

"Secret friend, I like that," says Catalpa, smiling at him.

Have any of the parents noticed that Catalpa's all googly-eyed over their couchsurfer? Sumac wonders.

The rule for Kris Kringle is, when it's your turn you can either open the wrapped present you're given, or steal one that's already been opened, but either way, you have to guess who the Secret Santa is who made that present, if you want to keep it.

Sumac happens to be Wood's Kris Kringle this year, so she's made a phone pouch for him out of three colors of leather. Earth colors, for Wood, of course — brown, gray, and green. It's been really hard to use the awl that makes holes in leather, and the needle's hurt her fingers, and it's taken weeks of hiding in her room.

"Nice," says Wood. He puts his phone into the pouch, to check it fits, then takes it out again.

"What's your guess, who made it?" asks PopCorn.

Wood doesn't even hesitate: "Catalpa."

Sumac's cross face gives it away.

"Whoops, was it you?" Wood asks her. "Really? That's amazing work."

She's not comforted. "Well, you don't get to keep it, because you guessed wrong."

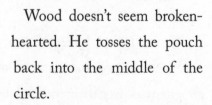

Wood doesn't seem broken-hearted. He tosses the pouch back into the middle of the circle.

"Sumac's turn," Brian says urgently.

(Which must mean that Brian's her Kris Kringle.)

What Sumac unwraps is . . . a bookmark. A pretty bizarre one, with doll feet glued at a funny angle to a long rectangle, so when you shut the book over it, it looks like you've flattened the doll inside.

"Guess who?" cries Brian.

"Hm," says Sumac, looking from face to face, trying to make it seem like she has no idea.

"Who be your Kiss King?"

"Kris Kringle," says Sumac. "Let's see. I wonder if it was . . ." She turns toward CardaMom as if she's going to guess her.

"Nah," says Brian, scathing.

"Could it be . . ." Sumac bends to look Oak in the eye suspiciously.

"Nah," cries Brian.

"OK, I'm going to guess —"

"Me!" Brian roars. "It was me!"

"No way," says Sumac. "*You* made this incredible book-mark with feet?"

"Yeah! Only PopCorn holded the glue gun," Brian adds resentfully.

Just as well, Sumac thinks, because last time Brian did

some hot-gluing, she burned Catalpa's elbow, and maybe not quite accidentally.

When the presents are all given out — and in the end Wood does get the phone pouch Sumac made, because nobody else is mean enough to swipe it — Catalpa says she's cold to the bone.

"What can we play that'll warm us up?" asks CardaMom.

The Lotterys try Balloon Badminton (slapping an inflated balloon off the floor and walls), which works pretty well until Aspen smacks it against a chandelier and bursts it with a bang that makes Oak cry.

Then they have a go at House Pong, which is like table tennis but without a table. Aspen and Wood manage a record-breaking rally of seventeen shots against the walls, furniture, floor, ceiling, and their own bodies before Topaz steals the Ping-Pong ball and takes it under a bookshelf to play with, and nobody can find another.

"Anyone want to try some aikido?" offers MaxiMum.

She has a regular sparring partner, Joe — the kids call him Ikey-Joe because he does aikido — but he hasn't been able to make it to Camelottery during the ice storm, so MaxiMum is itching for some practice. She wears special wide black pants and a white wraparound jacket, but the rest of them just make sure they've got stretchy things on.

226

Down in the Gym-Jo, they clear away the four sleeping bags. "Oh, so you didn't camp in the Ravine last night, then?" Sumac asks Wood.

He makes a horrible face at her, even though she was just asking. "CardaMom said somebody might call Child Protection Services if they saw me heading off to bed down in the snow."

After bowing and stretching and breathing exercises, the Lotterys *take ukemi*, which means practicing breakfalls: You drop on purpose, taking most of the impact with your arms or legs. Sumac likes the rolling ones best. There's one where you step forward with your right foot, and roll from your right shoulder to your left hip, and if you do it right, you feel like a marble spinning around in a cup.

Wood doesn't concentrate very well because he keeps staring at the wooden *tantō* (knife) on the wall, the *bokken* (sword), the *jō* (stick), and the *yari* (spear). "When do we get to use a weapon?"

MaxiMum grins at him. "I prefer 'empty hand' techniques, especially for beginners."

They're really just a cool collection, then, like Sumac's dolls. Sumac's favorite is the long sword with mother-of-pearl decorations. "Hey," she asks, "can you show us the heaven-and-earth throw?"

"Sure," says MaxiMum. "I'll do it with PopCorn, to

227

show it works even on people who are heavier than your-self." She gestures to him to attack her.

PopCorn moves in warily . . .

MaxiMum sweeps one hand low and the other high, knocking PopCorn off balance and flipping him right over on the mat; it's like some elegant dance move.

The kids all cheer and PopCorn tries to grin.

Aikido's like judo because you use the enemy's energy against them, but it's extra honorable because you make sure *they* don't break anything either. Sumac herself has never got as far as throwing anyone, but MaxiMum finishes her demonstration by tossing Wood halfway across the room.

"Excellent fall," she tells him. "Much better than your dad's."

"If you make yourself relax," Wood says, getting up, "it doesn't really hurt."

"I prefer swords," Brian tells Wood.

"Me too."

"I do swords with ice."

"I saw some epically long icicles hanging off our eaves troughs," he says, jumping up. "Let's have a tournament."

So the kids all wrap up well and stand around in the hall for ages while Brian ("No helping!" she keeps saying) gets her boots on. They go outside, skirting around the fallen pine branch and the *Caution Do Not Cross* tape. It's gray out, and every pole and fence spike and leaf is still varnished with ice.

The kids carefully break the longest icicles they can find off whatever pipe or car they're dangling from. Brian likes polishing hers, and lining them up against the front wall of Camelottery to make what she calls a sword shop. Wood and Aspen are fighting already, and they've smashed two swords each. "Poke, don't slash," Catalpa advises them.

Wood spots Mr. Rostov with his axe, and goes across the road to ask for a try at splitting logs.

"Fight me," Brian tells Sumac.

So they try a duel, with Sumac being very careful . . . but as soon as Brian waves her sword it crumples, leaving her with nothing but a stump. She bursts into furious tears.

"It's an interesting experiment," says Sumac, "because we learn that maybe water isn't the best thing to make weapons with."

"You broked it," growls Brian.

"I didn't even touch it," Sumac points out. "Gravity broke it."

"Gabbity's my friend, you're not my friend!"

Sumac gives up and goes off to join Aspen.

Brian starts using her icicles as spears and throwing them at Sumac, but luckily they don't travel very far.

Once the kids go back inside, bad temper starts to build up like poison gas in the freezing house. Especially once the phones and tablets start running out of juice. When Wood can't check how his clan's doing since the battle, and Catalpa can't text her friends, they get distinctly irritable.

Aspen keeps chasing Topaz to use her as a hand warmer, till the cat loses patience and scratches Aspen's wrist.

Even Luiz is not quite his sunny self today. He keeps wiping his eye and saying he thought it would have stopped dripping and itching by now.

Sumac's tummy rumbles. She turns to look at her parents. "I'm just asking: What are we going to do for Christmas dinner?"

The adults look at each other blankly. "Hm. Probably some delicious Bits 'n' Bobs?" says PopCorn.

A chorus of groans from the kids.

"If you think cross-culturally," says CardaMom, "anything can be Christmas dinner."

"I believe the Japanese like deep-fried chicken and strawberry cream cakes," says MaxiMum.

"In South Africa," supplies PopCorn, "the traditional Christmas dish is fried caterpillars of the emperor moth."

"Not eating *moths*," says Brian, disgusted.

"Oh, or what about kiviak?" suggests CardaMom.

"What's kiviak?" Aspen asks.

"It's a winter specialty in Greenland. Inuit people hollow out a seal —"

"Ew," squeals Aspen.

"— and stuff it with about five hundred auks — small birds. Close it up with fat, bury the whole thing for several months till it's decomposed, and then open it up, take out the birds, pop the head off each, and suck out its liquidized insides."

The kids howl and stagger around, pretending to retch.

"So I gather you'd prefer some delicious Bits 'n' Bobs, then?" asks CardaMom.

"Surely we can call for a pizza, or Thai food?" suggests Catalpa. She's standing in the open door, with fresh eyeliner on. "Unless you want us to *starve*?"

PopCorn meets MaxiMum's eyes and starts laughing.

MaxiMum says to him, "I seem to remember a moment about fifteen years ago when we all agreed *not* to raise our kids as arrogant, entitled little emperors and empresses . . ."

"We're just cold. And starting to get really hungry as well," says Sumac in a shaky voice.

"Hangry," says Wood, correcting her. That means hungry slash angry.

"Hirritable and hexhausted," says PopCorn comically. "Well, let's get the Gym-Jo all ready for the lot of us to sleep in tonight, and then we'll order some takeout, if anywhere's open."

"Let's bring all the rugs and cushions and duvets and pillows down to the basement," suggests CardaMom. "It'll be like one giant Mongolian yurt!"

When Aspen drags (not carries) the rugs down the stairs, she raises so much dust (because various Lotterys haven't been vacuuming very well) that Grumps has a coughing fit.

On top of the rugs the Lotterys spread spare blankets and duvets. Catalpa flops down and says, "That's it, I'm done."

MaxiMum claps her hands once, commandingly. "Come on, everyone fetch a sleeping bag from the closet in your room. This ship won't sail without all hands on deck."

"It's not a ship," says Catalpa, "it's a dark, squalid bed pit."

Sumac toils upstairs to fetch her sleeping bag. Bits of it feel glued together with . . . could it be burned marshmallow? She remembers now: Aspen borrowed Sumac's sleeping bag when she had two friends over for a campfire sleepover in August. She picks at the marshmallow with numb fingertips. Disgusting!

Secretly Sumac's half wishing she, Aspen, and MaxiMum had stayed in the Warming Center. They've lost their places now; if they went back, they'd probably find it full.

"Why've you got a puss on, missy?" Grumps asks her on the stairs.

Puss is a Scottish word for a sour expression, as if you have a nasty little cat sitting on your face.

"Oh, it's just that ... these holidays have gone so wrong," Sumac tells him. "The ice storm's messed everything up."

"What everything?" he asks.

"Like, half our traditions — going to *The Nutcracker*, you know, that ballet with the Sugar Plum Fairy? The 'ding ding ding ding' tune?"

Sumac didn't really think Grumps would recognize it from a few notes, but he nods. "Never could stand that one. The choir I played piano for back in Yukon, they insisted on doing selections from *The Nutcracker* every bloomin' winter. With handbells," he adds disgustedly.

"Well, I love it," says Sumac, her voice wobbling.

"And you'll see it again next year, no doubt," says Grumps. "By my age you'll be sick to your back teeth of ding-a-dings. In the meantime, whining like a babby won't change the weather."

Sumac stiffens, remembering how much she disliked

her grandfather when he first moved in with them last summer. She goes past him without another word.

Down in the basement, she spreads out her crusty-with-marshmallow sleeping bag. She has to be helpful, she reminds herself; she mustn't pick fights on Christmas Day. She racks her brains for some pleasant conversation to make.

"I have a seasonal joke," she announces.

No response. Everybody's busy preparing their kind-of-beds.

"Want to hear it?" Sumac asks, with a sharp edge to her voice.

"Want an honest answer?" mutters Catalpa.

"Yes, of course we want to hear it," says MaxiMum. "Go ahead, Sumac."

"I love the jokes," Luiz assures her.

Sumac is encouraged. "Knock knock."

"Next time," says Catalpa out of the side of her mouth, "just start with *knock knock*, and we'll probably manage to deduce that it's a joke."

"Knock knock," repeats Sumac stubbornly.

"You said that already," says Catalpa.

"You have to say, *Who's there?*" Sumac points out.

"Right," says MaxiMum, attaching another layer of bubble wrap over the windows with duct tape. "Who's there?"

234

"Who's there?" Luiz chimes in.

"Lettuce." Sumac waits.

Catalpa yawns theatrically.

"Lettuce who?" asks CardaMom.

"Lettuce in," says Sumac triumphantly, "it's freezing out here!"

A moment passes.

"Good one," says MaxiMum, but doesn't laugh.

"It's really not," says Catalpa.

"Is the joke over?" asks Luiz.

Sumac turns away, squeezing her lumpy pillow, because her eyes are prickling with tears.

"Sumac's never been able to tell a joke to save her life," says Catalpa to Luiz.

This pushes Sumac right over the edge. She spins around, the end of her pillow gripped in her two fists, and whomps Catalpa so hard with it she nearly knocks her over.

"What the — what the freak was that for?" screams Catalpa.

"You're so mean," Sumac screeches back.

"Hey hey, *amigas*," says Luiz.

"I'm not her *amiga*," roars Sumac, "I'm her sister, worse luck for me."

"No hitting," Brian sings out, pointing at Sumac. "You can't stay with the gang!"

"Oh, come on," protests Sumac. "Pillow fights don't count."

"For a pillow fight, you have to say, *Let's have a pillow fight*," says Catalpa stonily. "You can't just sneak up on someone and *assault* them."

"It's only feathers" — Sumac looks down to check — "or foam or something."

"My axe be foam and MaxiMum took it away," says Brian resentfully.

"Anyway," Sumac growls, "Catalpa so deserved it."

Catalpa looks like some old painting of a persecuted saint.

"That's not the point," says MaxiMum.

"Outside the room!" Brian's pointing.

Sumac looks at CardaMom, who hesitates, then nods.

She turns to PopCorn, who makes a sympathetic sad clown face.

"You guys are giving me a time-out, when I'm nearly ten?" asks Sumac in disbelief.

"Just for a few minutes. It'll help Brian learn the rule about hitting," murmurs CardaMom.

Sumac goes up to Catalpa and says in her ear, "Just so you know: I *know*."

Catalpa blinks at her. "What are you talking about?" But her face is going scarlet already.

236

Sumac's so tempted to say it out loud . . .

Catalpa and Luiz, up a tree
K-I-S-S-I-N-G!

. . . but no. That's not Sumac, even on her worst day.

She stomps out of the room and slams the door. Oh, she'll stay away from her whole wretched family for more than a *few minutes*.

The sun's setting now — at 4:46, which seems ridiculously early. The darkness is creeping back into the house. Sumac feels like an itchy, miserable, starving, white-fungal-nosed bat. These holidays are *un*salvageable. There's a certain relief in deciding that, and giving up on the whole mess.

She thumps all the way up to her room in the attic. She curls up on her bed and tries to read her graphic novel of *Les Misérables* by the very last of the daylight. Maybe learning about truly miserable people in nineteenth-century Paris will make her feel a bit less downtrodden by comparison?

It doesn't. Sumac sniffs a lot.

Then she spots her festive calendar; somebody's stashed it behind her bedroom door like a piece of junk.

She goes next door to the Artic and roots through the drawers for an extra big permanent marker (the kind the Lotterys use for signs at protest rallies). She puts a thick diagonal slash through all the fun things that haven't happened properly, or at all, or can't happen now. Sumac only got to see about half an hour of the Solstice Parade before they had to rush to the hospital with Luiz, and not the big burning at the end. PapaDum and Sic haven't come home *at all*. No dim sum. A Christmas tree like something out of a horror film, no good presents, and a Polar Bear Plunge that was the bravest thing Sumac's ever done but *no video evidence*. And finally, without PapaDum to bake or electricity to bake with, there'll be no Cookie Party tomorrow. Cancel it. Sumac's permanent marker slices through the word *Party*. Cancel everything.

Sumac gives her calendar a hard kick. The kind of kick that would make someone double over with bleeding innards, the kind she'll never let herself give any real person in her entire life.

The calendar couldn't care less. It's sturdy cardboard, so it just bounces smugly and falls to one side.

Sumac takes a pair of scissors and stabs it.

That's a bit better, because the calendar feels hard and makes a satisfying raggedy gasp. But still, she's only cut a small hole that you'd barely notice.

She tries to scissor right through the cardboard, and for a few centimeters it goes well, but then . . . the scissors fall apart at the hinge. Curses! That's pathetic. Sumac's favorite art scissors. How can steel be weaker than cardboard?

What she'd really like to do is burn this thing to a crisp.

Her eyes fall on the old cigarette lighter (*Pride Toronto 2007*) the Lotterys use for making things like wax drip paintings. She picks it up and practices flicking the flame on.

If it were summer Sumac would burn her calendar in the fire pit in the Wild behind the house. Obviously she's not going to set fire to a big square of cardboard indoors . . .

She runs over to the window and winches it to its widest point, letting in freezing air. (Luckily they had the attic windows replaced with triple-glazed ones last year, because Sumac would never have managed to get one of the old storm windows out of its slot.)

She looks down at the darkening yard, with the last streaks of sunset behind the trees. Then she sticks the calendar right out the window.

Sumac remembers how impossible it was to get her birthday candles to stay lit on the beach last May, when there was only a puff of wind. Tonight it doesn't feel as if there's any breeze at all, but she's shaking so much now, with cold or excitement, she can't tell. She makes a flame on the fourth try and holds it to the bottom edge of the calendar, where it says *Cookie Party*.

The cardboard edge blackens in a satisfying way, and then fire springs up. Success!

Sumac tilts the square of cardboard horizontally, so her hand won't get scorched. Her arm's tired, but she doesn't care. She braces her elbow, and holds out her flaming calendar like a big protest sign to the universe that says: *Everything gets messed up. All the best-laid plans of mice and men, and it's just not fair!*

The calendar's burning splendidly now, crackling and spitting and shooting out its orangest flames. Sumac's enjoying herself. She's going to chuck the calendar down into the icy grass behind the house now. Let it fly and finally fizzle out like a firework. She gives it one big heave —

Not quite big enough. Her arm must have been too tired.

Sumac leans out so far, the window frame feels like it's going to chop her in half. Way, way below, the festive calendar is burning on the roof of the Derriere. Caught on the very edge of the shingled porch roof, balancing on the eaves trough, which is full of dry, crispy leaves.

Arghhhhhhhhhhhh!

That's what Sumac shouts in her head, but what comes out is just a faint little groan in her nose.

Think, think. Be a problem solver. There's a fire extinguisher on the shelf beside the hot-glue gun, but it's no good to Sumac, because the fiery calendar is too far down to reach.

Pour water from the window?

She runs to fill a plastic bowl from the sink of the Rainforest, one floor down. If she bumps into anyone she'll ask for help, but she prays she won't, because this may be the stupidest thing she's ever done in her entire life.

Nobody's around. Probably all downstairs arguing some more.

The water slops over the rim as Sumac hurtles back up to the attic floor. Into the Artic and over to the open window. She leans out as far as she can go. The calendar's still flaming away. Has the house caught fire yet? Sumac pours the water in a shaky stream . . .

It splashes on the roof of the Derriere and pours off it, just to the left of the calendar, barely spattering the edge of the flaming cardboard.

Arghhhhhhhhhhhhhhh double arghhhhhhhhhhhhhhh!

Time to confess.

Sumac thunders down through the dim, cold house. "Somebody," she wails, like Brian. "Somebody!"

MaxiMum steps out of her room so unexpectedly that Sumac crashes into her bony shoulder. "What's the problem?"

Hard to speak for tears and gulping. "I didn't mean to but I've set Camelottery on fire!"

Even through her misery, over the next five minutes, Sumac is impressed by how unflappable her mother is. MaxiMum keeps her *isn't this an interesting experiment* tone throughout, even while she's dragging their stepladder upstairs from the Saw Pit and outside to position it on the ground just past the Derriere. Even as MaxiMum's climbing up (with Sumac holding the ladder extra steady) with the mop. Even as she's poking and levering the burning calendar with the mop handle until it floats down onto the ice-covered grass.

Steam goes up as the flames fizzle out. MaxiMum stamps out the last of the fire with her boot, until there's nothing but charred cardboard.

"Thanks so, so, so much," says Sumac in a wail. "But what about the roof?"

"Looks OK to me. These old mansions were built to last."

"I'm utterly sorry," she tells MaxiMum, her voice still choked.

Her mom grins at her. "There's one mistake you'll never make again."

"Was that your calendar thingy?" Aspen, balancing on the rail of the Derriere, sounds highly amused.

From inside, a faraway roar: "Shut the door!"

MaxiMum beckons the two girls back inside. Aspen scampers off to find the other Lotterys and tell them all.

"Hey," says MaxiMum to Sumac. "I know these holidays weren't exactly what you had in mind."

"I was only trying to help!" Sumac wipes her teary cheeks.

MaxiMum's forehead crinkles. "Help what?"

"You! You and PopCorn both seemed so stressed out, trying to manage without PapaDum, I thought I could . . . keep all our holiday traditions on track," she says weakly.

MaxiMum takes Sumac's hands and rubs them between her own to warm them up. "My love," she said, "sometimes things around here get a bit chaotic — even when there aren't any national emergencies — but that's all right, and it's not your job to fix it."

Sumac sniffs a few more times.

"Hey, can you guess what all this midwinter partying was about in the first place?" MaxiMum huffs hot air on Sumac's hands. "What scared our ancestors?"

Sumac so nearly says *dinosaurs*, which would lose her MaxiMum's respect forever, because of course humans and dinosaurs only shared the earth in cartoons. "Mammoths?"

she guesses instead. "Saber-toothed tigers? The cold? The dark?"

"Getting closer."

"They were scared . . . that winter would never end?"

"Bull's-eye," says MaxiMum. "All this singing and dancing and feasting, it was magic for bringing back the sun."

"Huh," says Sumac.

"Now you, my rational daughter," says MaxiMum, putting Sumac's palms on her own warm cheeks, "are you afraid the sun won't come back?"

"Nah," says Sumac. "It hasn't gone anywhere, it's just that the Northern Hemisphere's tilted away from it in winter."

MaxiMum nods. "Rituals are to make us feel safe. Do you feel safe?"

"Well, right this minute, yeah," says Sumac, grabbing hold of MaxiMum's long earlobes.

"Well, then." Her mother encloses her in a long, hard hug.

"We're going to do it every year!" That's Aspen, panting into the Mess.

"What's that?" asks MaxiMum.

"Sumac's big burn. Every Christmas Day, when it gets

dark, we're each going to write a list of our most epic fails — all the goals we forgot or didn't manage, or stuff we totally messed up during the year — and set our lists on fire and chuck them out the window! Not onto the roof of the back porch, obviously," Aspen says, "because, hello, that's a crime called *arson*."

"Such a therapeutic idea, Sumac!" says PopCorn, grabbing Aspen by the armpits and letting her dangle like a monkey. "Confronting the negative, which lets us clear a space for the positivity of New Year's resolutions."

"You know too many words," Aspen tells him over her shoulder.

"Well done on coming up with our newest tradition," MaxiMum tells Sumac.

Sumac lets out a little snort. "Not on purpose."

"Like many of the best inventions."

"Antibiotics, the microwave oven, sticky notes," chants Aspen. "They were all *acci-ventions*." She loves stories of scientists discovering things by mistake, because she's hoping to get through life without ever having to do any hard work.

The thump of the knocker resounds through the house. Aspen scampers off to answer the front door.

She's back in a minute, grinning ear to ear. "One of the

Marikkar twins from down the road — I think Ama, but it could be Anesha."

"What about her?" asks Sumac.

"Oh, yeah. She says can we come to dinner."

"Seriously?" asks PopCorn, so relieved his eyes bulge in the small circle of his flashlight.

CHAPTER 9

- -

FOOD, GLORIOUS FOOD

It's terribly dark with the streetlights out. The beams from their flashlights wobble about feebly. Grumps almost trips over the curb. PopCorn tries to use the flashlight app on his phone, but somehow turns on the antimosquito whine instead, which is no help. The Lotterys pick their way across

the icy road, bearing the few hostess gifts they've been able to rustle up in a quarter of an hour — a box of maple sugar sweets, and their Christmas pudding, which at least is already cooked.

PopCorn suddenly hisses, "Brandy!"

MaxiMum shakes her head. "The Marikkars are Muslim."

"Exactly, and the pudding's doused in brandy."

"Oh! Good save," MaxiMum tells him. She grabs the pudding from Sumac and hurries back to Camelottery.

The others crunch up the steps and ring the bell. And wait. Light is golden in the Marikkars' hall. "Eat and pass the dishes with your right hand, remember?" CardaMom tells the kids.

"But me and MaxiMum are lefties," says Wood.

"We'll manage," pants MaxiMum as she runs across the street to join them. "Sit on your left hand, if you need to."

The door opens.

"This is incredibly kind of you," PopCorn tells Mr. Marikkar in their warm hallway. "Inviting eleven extra people in, to eat you out of house and home."

"No problem at all," insists Mr. Marikkar, kissing PopCorn's cheeks. "You're most welcome. And your father! Good evening, Mr. Miller, sir."

CardaMom checks all the kids are taking their shoes off and leaving them on the rack by the door. Though Oak fights her, because he's got very attached to his penguin shoes. Grumps, it turns out, was still in his slippers, so he can stay in those.

Mrs. Marikkar's bump is looking even bigger, if that's possible. She gives each of the women and girls a hug and two kisses, but holds out her hand for PopCorn to shake.

"*As-salāmu 'alaykum*," he pronounces awkwardly. "Did I mess that up?"

"No, no, very good," she cries. "Peace be upon you all too."

There are other electricity-less waifs and strays in the hall already, Sumac sees. Mr. Tsering and Harry No Name, and three older men in white skullcaps like Mr. Marikkar's. Way more than eleven guests, then. What if they all really do eat the Marikkars out of house and home?

Sumac thinks she might be too embarrassed to swallow anything. It's *better to give than to receive*, and all that — but giving's also easier, she's discovered. It's way harder to be the peasant than the king.

But she shouldn't have worried about eating the

Marikkars out of house and home. When they walk into the dining room, she's never seen so much food in her life.

And that turns out to only be half of it. "Ladies, this way, please," says Mrs. Marikkar, beckoning CardaMom, MaxiMum, Catalpa, Aspen, and Sumac into the kitchen. There the daughters — four, no, all of them — are bustling around putting out another enormous spread. "But you guys aren't celebrating . . . I mean, today's nothing special for you, is it?" Sumac asks the eldest girl.

"Nah, Mom's just been cooking nonstop ever since the power outages started," says the girl ruefully. "This is the third night in a row she's invited neighbors in."

Sumac's impressed. She glances over her shoulder now to see Brian staying in the men's dining room, taking a seat between Grumps and (in his travel high chair that clips onto the table) Oak. But none of the Marikkars seem to object.

What about Grumps — what if he comes out with one of his awful remarks about *Arabs*?

The door closes, and Sumac realizes she can't do anything about what happens around the men's table now, which is kind of relaxing.

For a drink, Sumac can't decide between pomegranate

juice and a fizzy yogurt drink, but goes for the juice, as it's a safer bet.

"*Bismillah,*" says Mrs. Marikkar, eyes down.

That must be a kind of grace. Sumac shuts her eyes and thinks: *Thanks so much for a warm meal in a warm house instead of more wretched Bits 'n' Bobs!* Thinking about the *amigo secreto* game, she realizes something: The Marikkars are being the real secret friends today.

Mrs. Marikkar is bonding with Mr. Tsering's tired-looking, wheezing wife in a big way. It turns out they all got expelled from where they grew up (Sri Lanka in the case of the Marikkars, and Tibet for the Tserings). Expelled, like being kicked out of school, but not for doing anything wrong. "Two hours' warning only. With only the clothes we had on and fifty rupees in cash," Mrs. Marikkar murmurs, still wearing her perpetual smile, and passing dishes down the table.

Sumac tucks in to a sweet-and-sour fish curry with a fried flatbread called *paratha*, another curry called *polos* that she'd have sworn was beef but it turns out to be chunks of a fruit, candied pickled eggplant . . . and then she tries a little red chili called a cobra and her face nearly explodes, so she has to have a lot of plain rice to calm it down.

"You speak totes excellent English for somebody who isn't from here, Mrs. Marikkar," says Aspen.

That came out patronizing, so CardaMom gives her a look.

But Aspen thinks the problem is the slang. "Totally, is what I meant."

"This was eighteen years ago, my dear," says Mrs. Marikkar. "If you spend eighteen years in a new country, I hope you will speak that language well."

"Doubt it," mutters Catalpa.

Which isn't even fair, Sumac thinks, because Aspen picks up languages super fast: When the Lotterys went to Cuba on vacation, she was swapping greetings with strangers by day three.

Beside Catalpa, the smallest Marikkar jerks, and lets out a sob.

"Really sorry!" cries Aspen. "It was my sister I was trying to kick."

"Please excuse our overexcited children," says MaxiMum to Mrs. Marikkar. She turns her gaze on Aspen like a searchlight, and murmurs, "Would you rather behave in a civilized way, or wait outside in the cold?"

"Death threat!" mutters Aspen in protest. Then focuses on her plate.

"Did you know," says Sumac to Mrs. Marikkar, "fifty

percent of all the people in Toronto weren't born in Canada?"

"Really, dear, is it as high as that?" says Mrs. Marikkar.

"And fifty percent of my parents too, actually," Sumac tells her.

Here come the girls with the desserts: some kind of coconut egg pudding, another custardy one with cashews and raisins, crusty squares that are red or green or yellow . . . Sumac doesn't say a lot because she's now eaten so much that she's afraid if she opens her mouth she'll let out a massive burp.

The tea's served with hot milk: weird but not bad. Sumac holds her cup in two hands and soaks up the comfort of it, because she knows that any minute now the Lotterys will have to go back to their dark house where the temperature's still dropping.

It takes them ages to get their boots and coats on in the hall. Oak conked out at the start of dinner, according to Brian, and has been asleep on the sofa ever since.

"Oh, a wonderful pudding!" cries Mr. Marikkar.

What, another one? Sumac looks around for it.

"Bah, humbug!" counters PopCorn.

Ah, that's a Scrooge line, so they must be quoting *A Christmas Carol*. How nice that PopCorn's found another Charles Dickens fanboy to geek out with at last.

CardaMom scoops up their sleeping Oak and it's finally time to venture out into the freezing night. The Lotterys sing the "Food, Glorious Food" song from *Oliver!* all the way home.

✱

The cold air makes Oak wake up and sparkle, just when you'd expect him to be cranky. He insists on being put down, in his beloved penguin shoes, so he can stagger-walk (with one hand in PopCorn's and one in MaxiMum's) across the street.

"Shut the door, quick!" calls CardaMom as they hustle into the Hall of Mirrors.

Camelottery feels dead, somehow: silent, dark, and horribly chilly. How long will they be able to stay if the power's not fixed for weeks? Sumac wonders. Still, never mind about that for now, she decides; they just need to get through one night.

Brian's drooping, but she refuses to go to bed before her baby brother. "No lying down on the floor," she wails.

"It's not the Gym-Jo anymore, remember, it's our magical Mongolian yurt," Sumac tells her.

"Want my own bed in room with Oaky," protests Brian.

"Too cold up there," says CardaMom. "We'll be cozier down here."

"Not sleepy!"

They distract her by calling Gram — just a regular call, because she doesn't have a smartphone for Skyping — and shouting greetings down the line to Jamaica. There's raucous music in the background, because there's a Junkanoo parade going by.

Then they try Baba on the reserve. CardaMom tells him all about the ice storm. "He's boasting that the one that hit them in '98 was *way* worse," she reports when the call is over. "*Ten* centimeters of freezing rain, four *million* lost power, they had to send in the army . . ."

But that was before the kids were born, even. "It's not fair to compare," says Sumac. "This is the biggest disaster of my life."

The moms look at each other and laugh.

"What?" she demands. "What's so funny?"

"This is just weather," CardaMom tells her. "I'm pretty sure your life will include some bigger disasters."

"Great," said Sumac grimly. "I'll look forward to those."

"*Not* sleepy," says Brian again.

Which means she must be.

Sumac offers to get into pj's with her little sister and read her a book, as that usually does the trick. She brings her into the Nether Cesspit (their basement washroom) to brush their teeth over the little corner sink.

Of course it's never just one book. By the beam of a flashlight, Sumac reads Brian an Anna Hibiscus one, about the girl in Nigeria who has baby brothers called Double and Trouble.

Sumac scratches her head through her wooly hat. Weird to be wearing hats in bed, but apparently that's the key: Don't let any heat escape out of your head.

Next Brian picks *The Seven Silly Eaters*, which she likes because it's the same number of kids as the Lotterys.

Except that their big silly Sic is missing, of course: having Christmas with the other construction volunteers in a hostel under a decorated banana tree, eleven thousand kilometers away.

The picture blurs. Sumac blinks, and two hot drops fall on the page.

"No wetting me book," says Brian crossly, and takes it away from Sumac, to wipe with her pajama sleeve.

Well, that's killed the mood. So Sumac gives Brian a kiss on the wooly hat she's got on under her earmuffs, and turns off the flashlight.

"On!" protests Brian.

"OK, I'll leave it on the lower setting," says Sumac, "but no playing games with it. You need to sleep."

"OK."

"No shadow pictures, OK?"

"I said OK," says Brian, but she's crossing her fingers. "Where Oaky?"

"He'll be down soon. Time to snoozle," suggests Sumac. "When you wake up we'll all be here, all sleeping together in the magical yurt."

"When do butts crack?" asks Brian.

"What?" asks Sumac, bewildered.

"Has they always a crack?"

"Yeah, we're born that way. Otherwise how could the poop get out?" Sumac tries to untangle herself from the duvet without letting a draft in. . . .

Brian's hard little fingers close on her ankle. "You stay."

"OK, just for a little."

To keep warm while she's waiting for Brian to drop off, Sumac burrows down under the layers.

The next thing she knows, it must be late that night. Beams bob around the room, and there's a lot of giggling. Grumps says something about falling down a hole in the blackout during the war.

Thump: That sounded like someone walking into the wall . . . "Ow!"

"Drunkard," MaxiMum says affectionately.

PopCorn sounds as if he's in pain. "You're the one who hangs lethal Japanese weapons all over the walls."

"Shh. You'll wake the wee ones."

Sumac wants to say that she's not a wee one, she's almost ten. But if she doesn't speak, she can tell herself she's still asleep, and dive back down down down . . .

"Argh!" She sits up.

Wood has the nerve to shush her.

"You stood on my stomach," Sumac hisses.

"So that's what felt so gooey."

"*Boa noite* everybody," whispers Luiz, "sleep good!"

He sounds a bit muffled too. Probably because he's face-down on his ramp thing, Sumac realizes. Luiz hasn't *slept good* all week, but he manages to sound so cheerful.

"Are those your teeth chattering, Reginald, you big softy?" asks Grumps.

"Yeah," admits PopCorn. "It's a tad cold in here, Dad!"

The old man snorts. "It's far from central heating I was raised. Our water would freeze in the glass. We were a tougher generation."

"Agreed, no contest," says PopCorn through a yawn, "you survived Nazi bombing raids. Night, Dad."

The cold wakes Sumac early. Where is she this time? In the Gym-Jo, that's right. She snuggles down again, and tries to persuade herself that she's still dreaming. But sleep's one of those things that you really can't *try* to do, because if you're trying, you're not relaxing, so you're not falling asleep. *Come on, muscle of surrender!*

It's Boxing Day, though Sumac's not sure why it's called that: In the old days when there was no TV or sales in malls on the twenty-sixth, did they entertain themselves with boxing matches? In South Africa they call today the Day of Goodwill, she remembers.

A heave of the bedclothes. Brian clambers out and stumbles out of the room, leaving the door of the Gym-Jo open to the colder air.

Usually Sumac would be leaping out of bed this morning to help PapaDum with his last few batches for the Cookie Party. Last year, Aspen *acci-vented* a new variety when she misread *½ cup butter* as *1½ cups*. The cookies came out as sizzling puddles, but once they set they were so delicious, and Aspen named them Utterly Butterlies.

Which gives Sumac an idea . . .

"Mr. Marble!" From the Nether Cesspit next door, Brian's shriek resounds through the house.

MaxiMum sits bolt upright. "Brian? What is it?"

"I poke my poop with the fork," calls Brian through the wall, "and here's Mr. Marble! Want to see him?"

"No," the two mothers shout simultaneously.

"Somebody?"

"Nobody wants to see the marble. Wash it — and your hands," says MaxiMum.

"With lots and lots of soap," adds CardaMom.

That's it for any chance of getting back to sleep. Sumac wriggles out of her sleeping bag like an insect shedding its skin.

A loud flush and the running of water. Brian comes in with dripping hands and a proud expression. "See?" She holds up the marble. "He's the same exact."

"Excellent," groans CardaMom.

"He comed right down through me and — plop!"

"Clever Mr. Marble," says MaxiMum.

"Clever me," says Brian, rubbing her tiny belly.

Shivering up in the Mess, Sumac goes to turn on the tablet — forgetting that it's dead. OK, she can do this old-school, with paper and markers. Because remembering the Utterly Butterlies has given her a great idea. Sumac can do lateral thinking if she sets her mind to it; in fact, she can be just as bendy-brained as Aspen.

Neighbors! We Lotterys are SO sorry
our stove has no power so we can't
throw our usual Cookie Day party.
But–

It occurs to her that she'd better get a parent's OK before she uses up all her red and green on the invitation.

When Sumac goes back down to the basement, CardaMom's not there and MaxiMum's meditating, face to the wall. Better not bother her.

PopCorn stirs, under about three duvets. His eyes are shut, but that doesn't mean he isn't half-awake at least.

Sumac whispers her plan in his ear.

He moans a little bit, and presses his head into the pillow.

"So can I go ahead?" she says in his other ear.

"Knock yourself out, Sumac." PopCorn's voice is slurred, but he did say her name, which means he's conscious enough.

So she runs back to the Mess to finish the invitation.

But since our street has no traffic on it right
now anyway,
why don't we all have a
Cookie Swap Street Party?

263

See you outside our house at 12,
and please bring cookies if you've
got any in the cupboard!

How to make multiple copies is the problem: If Sumac has to write all the invites out by hand, Boxing Day will be over before she's done . . .

She catches Wood in the Hall of Mirrors, about to take Diamond out, and surprisingly enough he agrees to go as far as the convenience store to photocopy the invitations.

By noon, miraculously, it's all come together. MaxiMum and various neighbors have set folding tables out in the street, and there are tall juice dispensers, two big boxes of coffee, and a giant thermos (from Mr. Rostov) of strange, minty hot chocolate. Mr. Tsering's brought a bottle of something called ice wine that's made by crushing frozen grapes.

It looks like everyone who lives on this block is here. Somebody's old boombox is resting on a gatepost, and kids are dancing to Drake and Miley Cyrus. There are Moroccan sesame pretzels, Dutch *speculaas* shaped like birds and cats and elephants, cinnamon snickerdoodles, Norwegian

cream-filled *krumkakes*, something called *ma'amul* stuffed with pistachios. Linzer cookies with hearts of jam, honey-dipped ginger *yak kwa* from Korea . . . it's amazing.

Aspen and Sumac go around quietly awarding prizes for Most Artificial-Looking (bright pink cardboardy wafers), Most Creepy (Grumps has contributed a pack of his private stock of squashed fly biscuits), Best Name (spicy iced *pfeffernüsse*), and Worst Idea (charcoal biscuits from England with actual charcoal in them). They try to decide on Tastiest but they can't agree, so they keep testing more and more cookies till they feel sick.

Mr. Rostov arrives with a massive gingerbread house — glued together with still-gooey icing, as if by a drunken builder. The smaller kids enjoy demolishing that. Then they use up their energy at PopCorn's Decoration Station, taking plain cookies from a box and adding way too much spray-on icing, sparkles, and jellies.

Luiz says Mrs. Marikkar's *ghorayeba* — cookies with a whole almond in the middle — remind him of *biscoitos de maizena* from home. "I have long."

"You have long what?" asks Sumac. "Long biscuits?"

He tries again. "I long for it."

"For an almond biscuit? Oh, you mean *home*," says Sumac. "You're missing home."

"Yes, and my many family."

"Why don't you go back, then, once your eye's better?" Sumac suggests.

Luiz grins and shrugs at the same time. "But I like to see the world first."

Harry No Name arrives with a packet of maple leaf creams, which he insists are the most famous Canadian cookies.

Sumac's never had one, or even heard of them.

"Guess you guys are too fancy-shmancy, with your organic kale and all that," he says with a snigger. "Oh well, it takes all sorts."

Even the emergency crew who are dealing with the fallen wires around Camelottery take a break and have a few cookies with their coffee. "Gluten-free?" CardaMom's saying to one woman. "Go for the Arabian coconuts — nothing but coconut, powdered milk, and sugar."

Finally, the best thing, the sun comes out — or what Brian would call a slice of it, at least. Sumac stares up, shuts her eyes, and enjoys the glow through her lids.

"Hey, what if we do it this way from now on?" says MaxiMum, beside her.

"You mean —"

"Everyone brings a packet to share," says MaxiMum, "instead of PapaDum having to wear himself out over the holidays baking six million different cookies to prove we're the big shots of the neighborhood."

Sumac can see what she means. She hates to admit it, but this kind of party's even better: more togetherish. "His quadruple chocolate cookies are still going to be the best, though."

"No question," says MaxiMum.

✱

"*Adeus*," roars Luiz in the hall that afternoon. "*Adeus*, Lotterys!"

All the family members within earshot thump through the house. "What," says Sumac, "are you going already?" She counts in her head: Yeah, this is the fifth day.

"Doctor Yazdani gave him the all clear," Carda-Mom reports. "She was particularly impressed to hear about all the facedown convalescent equipment Catalpa improvised."

Catalpa purses her lips crossly. "You still have to use the timer on your phone every six hours, to remind you to spend fifteen minutes looking down," she tells Luiz. "Right, *senhor*?"

"Right," he says, saluting like a soldier.

"Are you allowed to sleep flat now?" Sumac wants to know.

"Yes," says Luiz excitedly. "But on my side, not my back."

Sumac wonders how he's meant to remember that in his sleep; doesn't everybody roll around in the night?

"But what he's not allowed at all is to go anywhere very high up," CardaMom reports.

"So I totally change my plans," says Luiz. "No France for ski. I go by train, four days, across Canada to Vancouver. I see your lovely country all the way!"

"For a goodbye present, Luiz — we've got you a ticket that includes meals and a bunk to sleep in," says PopCorn, presenting the envelope with a little bow.

"Too super!"

"Well, it seemed cruel for you to have to spend three days sitting upright in your train seat," says PopCorn, "now you've finally got permission to lie down."

"Where to, after Vancouver?" asks Sumac.

"Who knows? I go with the flow." Luiz flips her sniffly, cold nose with his finger. "I'm just happy to be off to my travel."

But Sumac persists. "What about when your shrunk money runs out?"

"I find some job then," says Luiz with a shrug. "No worries."

"Sumac," CardaMom murmurs, "let him be."

It's a pity Luiz isn't likely to ever be giving birth, Sumac decides, because his muscle of surrender is extra strong.

"Taxi's here," says MaxiMum, looking out the door.

"Lotterys! You fix my eyeball," Luiz declares to them all, pointing to his eye. His hand moves down. "You feed my stomach." And up again. "And my heart. My Canada *familia*!" He starts a round of double kisses and long embraces.

Oak tries to give him a kiss, but he doesn't have the order quite right: He smacks his lips together on the approach, then opens them wetly as he plants his face against Luiz's.

"Are we ever going to see you again?" Sumac wonders aloud.

"For surely," says Luiz. "One way or another, somewhere or otherwhere."

"Slate wants to say bye-bye." Aspen holds him out.

Luiz recoils just a little, then says, "Bye-bye, rat." He manages to stroke Slate's glossy back with one fingertip.

When it's Catalpa's turn for a hug, she squirms out of his reach. "I hate goodbyes. Go pick coconuts!" she adds gruffly. She shoves something small into his hand. "Made this for your trip."

Sumac pushes near enough to read the button over Luiz's shoulder. It says — in big letters cut out of a newspaper, like a ransom note — *Always Talk to Strangers*.

270

"*Obrigado*, thank you," cries Luiz, letting out one of his most honking laughs. "I love it —"

But Catalpa's already turned on her heel.

The Brazilian's eyes follow her as she runs up the stairs. "Skype me? See you someday at Rio!"

They all hear the door to her Turret slam.

"Rude!" murmurs Aspen.

But Sumac knows that's not it.

Luiz is pinning the button to his big backpack. MaxiMum, toting his pack, hurries him out the door.

Only then does Sumac notice PopCorn's latest quote scrawled on the long mirror that's framed with little log slices. It looks at first glance like

Me dinate is whet we expel;
The walker is that we set.

But she finally figures out his awful handwriting.

The climate is what we expect;
The weather is what we get.

Sumac wanders upstairs, making dragon breaths and rubbing her mittens together to warm her hands. She hesitates outside Catalpa's medieval door.

She can hear the sobbing. Catalpa — so cool, so cynical — is breaking her heart in there.

If it was Brian, Sumac would go in and try to comfort her. But she knows she's better off staying out of this.

Could Luiz have figured it out? You don't need to be fluent in the same language to notice what someone feels. Yeah, maybe Luiz knew, and was tactful enough not to let Catalpa know he'd guessed about her crush.

A funny thing occurs to Sumac: Five years probably isn't much of a gap later on, the way it is now. Maybe someday when Catalpa's an adult, she will get to Rio, and meet Luiz again . . .

Ye ancient doore suddenly opens. Sumac leaps back — but it's obvious that she's been standing here, eavesdropping.

Face puffy, Catalpa scowls at her. But doesn't ask what Sumac's doing. "My contacts are really bugging me." She wipes one streaming eye.

Sumac nods. "That must be awful." Then she says, "Sorry about the pillow."

"What? Oh," says Catalpa wearily, as if she'd forgotten all about yesterday's fight. "Yeah, whatever."

Well, that wasn't the most gracious way to accept an apology, thinks Sumac, turning away.

"It's PapaDum and Sic," PopCorn calls from the hall.

Sumac squeals and dashes downstairs . . .

But of course he doesn't mean here and in person, only on a video call. Still. Sumac grins into the phone and waves — in slo-mo, so the image won't blur.

"How's the power outage?" calls Sic.

"Brutal," Sumac shouts back. "We can't feel our fingers or toes."

"You can't what?"

"Fingers and toes. They're blue!" Sumac takes off her gloves to wiggle them.

PapaDum leans in to the camera, frowning. "Isn't the generator working?"

Nobody says anything for a second.

"Sorry, what generator do you mean?" asks PopCorn.

"Is that them?" asks CardaMom as she comes through the hall. "*Kwe*, sweeties!"

"PapaDum's saying something about a generator," Sumac tells her.

"What generator?" That's CardaMom.

"*Our* generator," says PapaDum on the little screen.

"You don't mean —" PopCorn claps his hands over his face.

"The backup generator I bought about five years ago, in case of emergencies." PapaDum sounds unusually stern.

"Hon — why didn't you tell us?" said PopCorn.

"Of course I told you," roars PapaDum. "You can't have been listening. Besides, what did you all think that big machine sitting in the back of the shed was?"

"Whoops. I don't think I've ever gone to the back of the shed," says CardaMom.

"You're all as bad as each other!"

"Happy Christmas to you too, my friend," says CardaMom, blowing him a kiss.

"Go wheel the generator around to the side of the house this minute, and plug it into the receptacle that connects to the transfer switch," PapaDum orders.

"Right," says PopCorn. "The receptacle." Then, looking to the left, then the right, he asks, "Ah, which side of the house would that be, darlin'?"

Sumac runs off to tell the others that soon they'll be able to have heat and at least some lights and the microwave and kettle, and can charge their electronics. "Good news," she roars. "Hear ye the good news!"

That afternoon, the Lotterys finally remember their Christmas pudding, and retrieve it from behind the tree in the Hall of Mirrors where MaxiMum stashed it. PopCorn microwaves it, then sets some brandy on fire in a ladle and pours it over, so the whole dome burns blue under its holly crown. They all clap and cheer.

CardaMom gets the thimble for luck in life, Brian gets the coin for luck in wealth, and Wood gets the ring for luck in marriage (but swaps it with CardaMom because he swears he'd rather defenestrate himself than marry anyone). Sumac gets nothing, but that's all right.

Oak crushes a bit of pudding in his fingers, then rubs his head with it.

"Oaky!" Catalpa wails in protest.

He grins and sucks his whole fist like a big cake pop.

Sumac only has a tiny slice and doesn't finish it. "I've never actually liked Christmas pudding, just the smell of the spices."

"After all that effort of making it!" PopCorn puts on a pretend-offended face.

"But I love the feeling that people have been doing this just the way we're doing it, ever since the Middle Ages," she assures him.

"I hate to break it to you, but medieval Christmas pudding was a kind of soupy beef porridge," he tells her. "*Mincemeat*, as in, minced-up meat."

"Ew!"

Wood and Aspen announce that they have a surprise for

the family. "It's like a mini Highlights Reel, but just of the holidays," Aspen explains, turning on the tablet.

Sumac is about to get offended that they swiped her video-editing job . . . then decides to go with the flow.

Wood puts on a deep movie-trailer voice: "We call it: Festive Fails."

With a high-pitched circus clown soundtrack, the slide-show begins:

The Manitoba maple pressed up against the
    Marikkars' house.
A close-up of the watermelon Brian dropped on the
    floor.
A close-up of Luiz's damaged eye, all red and horrible.
A photo of PopCorn's pumpernickel pistachio bread.

"Oy," he protests over the music. "It wasn't a fail, it just had an unusual flavor."

The slideshow carries on.

A few lingering, repulsive seconds of Aspen biting a
    toenail.
A screenshot of the Toronto airport website, with
    Canceled after every flight on the list.
A close-up of small tooth marks in MaxiMum's arm.

276

Instead of being embarrassed, Brian boasts, "Mines!"

A hand-drawn sign that says YOUNGEST POLAR
    BEAR PLUNGE PARTICIPANT EVER? Due
    to technical difficulties, no video available.
A photo of the huge branch from the white pine, lying
    across the power lines it ripped down.
A few seconds of wavy, night-blurred footage of
    MaxiMum poking the burning calendar down off
    the eaves trough with a broom, while Sumac hovers
    beside her guiltily.
And finally, a picture of Brian's Mr. Marble.

"*Not* a fail," Brian protests.

"Bravo," cries PopCorn, clapping as the slideshow ends.
"*Bravissimo!*"

Brian lets out a shriek, and points at Oak.

He's walking away from his family, out of the Mess. Tilting left, with his butt stuck out, but still: actually walking, all by himself!

Brian shouts: "You walking, Oaky!"

He turns his head when he hears his name, and grins, and topples over. But doesn't even cry.

And the Lotterys all whoop and cheer.

*

It's after nine. Yawning, Sumac goes up and gets into her pajamas without anyone suggesting it. But she's left *Tuck Everlasting* in the Mess, so she comes back down for it.

In the Hall of Mirrors she glimpses Wood and CardaMom pulling on their boots over their snowpants, and Aspen rummaging so deeply in the basket that she's about to topple in headfirst. "Where are you all going at this time of night?" asks Sumac.

Aspen rights herself, with one tiny red glove and one enormous maple leaf Winter Olympics mitten. She's got a fleece tube pulled down over her eyebrows and another pulled up over her nose. "Nowhere," she says mysteriously.

"Liars!" says Sumac.

CardaMom seems to be hesitating.

Wood makes the zip-it gesture at their mother. "She's still in single figures."

"Nearly double," says CardaMom.

"What are you talking about?" Sumac demands.

"*Tsi't-ha*," CardaMom tells her, "there's one holiday thing you don't know about yet . . ."

She's furious: What right do her family have to hush-hush traditions?

"Because you're only nine, and tiddling little

under-tenners can't come night skating on the pond," says Aspen smugly.

No way: the pond in High Park? "If maturity could be measured," says Sumac as nonshoutily and maturely as she can, "I'd have about twice as much of it as Aspen."

Aspen pretends to be stunned into silence, opening her mouth like a fish. But she can't actually deny it.

CardaMom jerks her head toward the stairs. "Run and get ready, then."

Sumac gallops up three flights to her room to pull on her snowpants, jacket, gloves, and snood over her pajamas. She's not feeling one bit sleepy anymore.

By the time she gets down to the hall again, MaxiMum's introducing Joshellynne their sometimes-sitter to Grumps. Joshellynne's got an interesting haircut this month — all buzzed on one side, and long enough to sit on on the other. "Well, my folks are pretty conservative," she explains, "so when I go stay with them I brush the long bit over the shaved bit, and then they don't have to see it."

Sumac's about to remind Joshellynne to check on Luiz too when she remembers that he's left already. She feels an odd pang. The Lotterys' couchsurfer, heading out into the world, to surf on other people's couches . . . She hopes his new hosts will be nice to him. And not break any other bits of him. And give him enough fruit.

Soon PapaDum and Sic will be home and everything at Camelottery will be *camelordinary* again. Sumac might almost be sorry the crisis is all over.

MaxiMum pulls on a balaclava that shows nothing but her smiling eyes. "Shall we?"

The Lotterys haul their fourteen ice skates along on a single sled, and only spill a couple at corners. It's quite hard going, on the sidewalk, because everyone's piled the storm debris outside their doors for the garbage crews to pick up at some point.

The brisk walk to High Park warms Sumac up. It's milder tonight.

"Could go above freezing point by tomorrow," says Wood. "Not that that'll do much good now. The city's lost a fifth of its trees," he adds grimly.

"It's a pity ice is fatter than water," Sumac mentions to MaxiMum, "because that makes cracks in the road every winter."

"Ah, but if water was like every other substance and contracted when it froze, instead of expanding, that would be the end of the world."

Sumac is appalled. "How come?"

"Well, ice would be heavier than water then, not lighter, so rivers and lakes would freeze and kill all the fish," says MaxiMum.

"I never thought of that."

Wood chimes in. "The polar ice would sink, and push up all the rest of the water, so there wouldn't be any dry land at all."

"I'm glad I'm not in charge of the universe," Sumac admits. "I don't know enough yet, so I might break it."

"Wait a few years before taking on that job, yeah?" suggests MaxiMum, laughing.

It's so strange to be here crossing this huge park instead of in her own bed, but Sumac finds she's not sleepy at all. The moon's a staring eye between the branches of a birch. Stars are scattered across the sky.

PopCorn's using an astronomy app to tell him where to find Orion and Cassiopeia, but when he trips over a bush, his family mock him so much he puts his screen away.

"Mint?" MaxiMum offers Sumac a tube.

She's suspicious: Parents pushing candy? "Do I have bad breath?"

"No, it's an experiment. Chew it."

Sumac takes one and bites.

"With your mouth open," says MaxiMum.

Curiouser and curiouser, as Alice says in Wonderland. Sumac chews.

MaxiMum opens her own mouth, working her jaws, and grins.

Sparks!

"Blue lights in your mouth, wowza!" cries Aspen.

"Actually, all sugar lets out a little light, mostly ultraviolet, when you crush it — the electrons bump into nitrogen molecules in the air," explains MaxiMum. "But oil of wintergreen is fluorescent, so it converts the ultraviolet into longer-wavelength visible —"

"Just gimme some, Mrs. Blah Blah," says Aspen, grabbing three mints.

"Tagged you," says Wood behind Sumac, jumping on her shadow with both feet.

So then the kids and MaxiMum play moon shadow tag and pretend not to be related to CardaMom and PopCorn, who are improvising harmonies on an old croony song called "Blue Moon."

The wreckage of the past week fills the park; a Pick-Up-Sticks of branches. But the evil sorceress's power is beginning to melt away, Sumac realizes. Goodbye and good riddance!

She can't really hate the ice storm, for all the harm it's done. She thinks of Grumps, with his holey brains, reminiscing about Christmas on the beach in 1966. Maybe things need to be odd or hard, to get burned into your memory? Maybe when Sumac's eighty-three, the holiday season she'll still be blabbing on about will be this one that went so wrong.

She feels sick with excitement as she's lacing up her skates at the edge of the frozen pond. It's vast, as irregular as a puddle of ink. Sumac's never skated on natural ice before, so she stays near enough to one parent or another, just in case. The pond is a bit rougher than a rink, and it lets out the odd frightening creak. Massive trees arch up all around its rim, and Sumac's relieved to see that so many of them have survived. Dogs yip from the thickest part of the woods. Or . . . "Those are dogs, yeah?" she calls to Wood.

He flashes his teeth in a grin as he zooms right at her and stops at the last moment, his blades slicing side-ways and spraying ice. "Coyotes."

"Oh."

Wood slides along beside her for a bit, but it just makes Sumac skate worse.

"A hundred years ago, they were still harvesting this," he says, with a wave all around.

"Harvesting what," asks Sumac, "the trees?"

"The ice. Before refrigeration, they plowed it, stacked it up in blocks, covered it with mounds of sawdust for insulation, and sold it right through the summer."

"Cool!"

"Literally." Wood cuts off to one side to chase PopCorn.

Back in the day, Sumac supposes, electricity was an

extra, whereas now it's hard to get through a day without it. She vows never to take it for granted anymore . . . though she knows she will.

Sumac tries to memorize this cold, let it sink right into her lips, her cheeks, the bare bit of neck between her snood and her coat. Harvest the feeling. Next summer when she's all limp and sweaty, she'll close her eyes and conjure up this deep-down cold.

She works up some speed and practices her cross cuts, lifting her right foot over her left and shifting her weight as she rounds a corner. She realizes what's making her nervous: That scene in *Little Women* when Amy falls through the ice and her big sister Jo has to drag her out. "Catalpa?" she calls in a small voice when her sister floats by.

"What?"

"You know in *Little Women*?"

"What about it?" Catalpa spins from skating forward to backward to forward again; stylish. You'd never know she was heartbroken about a Brazilian she may never see again.

"Would you —" Sumac tries again. "Do you think, if the ice cracked, if I ever —"

Her sister snorts, reading Sumac's mind. "Nah, I'd leave you drowning in the hole." And flashes off into the dark.

Sumac decides not to believe her, and smiles.

She pushes on, and PopCorn's suddenly beside her, gliding backward. "Admit it," he says, "you've enjoyed these unconventional holidays."

Sumac makes a face.

"Come on! Kinda, sorta, lil' bit?"

"More or less," she mutters, and skates off into a patch of silver light.

THE THANK-YOU PAGE

A shout-out to Bruno, our wonderful guide (favelawalkingtour.com) in Rio's Rocinha, and Frederico Santos, Andreia Goncalves, and Mariana Martins Silva for catching many of my Brazilian errors: for those that remain, *desculpe!* I want to thank Roberta Duhaime for advice on Mohawk language and culture, and my dear friend Bipasha Baruah for being my India expert. To my wonderful editors, Arthur Levine, Suzanne Sutherland, and Venetia Gosling, and my agent, Caroline Davidson. To Torontonians (Elizabeth Ruth and Shannon and Violet Oliffe, Sheila Cavanagh, Richard Sanger and Debbie Lambie, James Tracy, Lauren Morocco, and *ma belle belle-mère* Claude Gillard), for sharing their urban enthusiasms. To Dr. Arjan Yazdani, and Sheldon, Desana, Seth, and Alex Rose, whose surnames I've gratefully borrowed. To friends who let me pick their brains about Buddhism (Margaret Lonergan) and adoption (Judy Core and Ange

Sumegi). And above all to Caroline Hadilaksono, for bringing the Lotterys to exuberant visual life.

Finally, thanks, my darling Roulstons, for inspiration on every page: Finn and Chris, and especially Una for being this book's first editor.